The Villagers

Dr Harrison Lane series

Preacher Boy

The Horsemen

Dark Order

Holy Man

Mermaid Rock

Blood Stone

Winter Fires

Hanging Tree

DI Claire Falle series

Lonely Hearts

Home Help

Death Bond

Published in 2022 by Chalky Dog Publishing

PLEASE NOTE: SPELLINGS USED IN THIS BOOK ARE BRITISH ENGLISH.

KEEP IN TOUCH

If you would like to keep in touch with Gwyn and hear about her latest releases, you can sign up for her free readers' newsletter, and receive an exclusive Harrison Lane novelette when you join.

The story tells how Harrison first started the Ritualistic Behavioural Crime unit. You'll be sent monthly book related news, offers, and competitions from Gwyn, but you can unsubscribe at any time.

Join Gwyn GB's readers' club at www.gwyngb.com/harrisonlane

BLOOD STONE

GWYN GB

CHALKY DOG
PUBLISHING

1

Carole Templeton shivered as she touched the rough grey granite of the stone. It was cold. The red sun was already on its way down, its bottom edge dipping into the dark grey sea to the west. Soon it would be extinguished and the darkness would envelop her. The easterly winds which raked the landscape in the winter months had settled into their role of reducing the 'feels like' temperature down by several degrees. She'd taken her gloves off, more in homage to her father than anything else, as though touching the stone and laying her bunch of flowers at its base would somehow appease the curse that had taken him. Not that she believed in curses, of course.

For the millionth time that week, she whispered into the air, asking him what had possessed him to try to uncover the secrets her great grandfather had always told them should remain buried. She'd heard the story so often as a child, sometimes with embellishment, but always the same facts. Her great grandfather had gone to Malaysia, taking two of the men from the village. The Templetons had been very wealthy in those days and he'd gone in search of exotic plants to add to their orangery. It was the defining characteristic of the house, running all along the western flank. Nobody knew what they'd found, but the facts were that somewhere on one of the islands in the Strait of Malacca, the men from the village were killed, and her great grandfather was lucky to escape with his life.

The blood stone had stood on the outskirts of the Templeton land for centuries. It was thought that at some point, it had been a pagan worship site. Somewhere that people would come and pay homage and give sacrifices to the glowing sun, which rose in front of them in the east and travelled across the vista until it sank below the western waves. The legend was that the stones protected the land and the people who lived on it, and it had got its name because at some time in the 17th century, a vampire had been buried beneath it. The village had been terrorised by the night walker who'd broken out of his coffin before burial and gone in search of blood. He'd wandered through the village at night banging on doors and howling, before being found seemingly dead again, in his bed in the morning. They'd taken him and buried him beneath the blood stone in order to stop him from rising again. It had worked. The villagers were never again terrorised by the vampire.

When Carole's great grandfather returned from Malaysia, rumours had spread that the men had been attacked and killed because he'd raided a holy temple. Although Henry had escaped, a curse had been put on him and his family. Her great grandfather had woken most nights in terror, screaming into the darkness but refusing to talk of what he'd seen. Finally, he'd taken some items he'd brought back from Malaysia, and he'd buried them beneath the blood stone, seeking its protection for his family. Only then did peace return to their lives.

Nobody knew what it was her great grandfather had buried, but there was talk that it was treasure worth a fortune and stolen from a once great Malacca empire. Gold that had lain buried for centuries and protected by the ancient curse. Had her father gone to dig it up in the hope it might help revive the family fortunes? Money was running out and her parents had been forced to sell off land in recent years. After a storm had damaged the roof last winter, she knew that they were contemplating selling even more land, but without land, there'd be no income from rent and farming, so it was a vicious circle. Carole had offered to give them some money to make the repairs. Her job in London paid well and as it was still just her, she'd only her mortgage to consider, but her father was a proud man. He'd refused her offer of help, and that of her brother's. She wished he hadn't because then he might still be alive and well at home with her mother.

The colour of the setting sun gave the big granite stone a red hue. The white crystals embedded within it reflected the sky and Carole wondered if perhaps this was the real reason why the stone had got its name, not because of some old folk tale.

Night was almost upon her, but the chill in the air wasn't just a physical one. Although the stones were supposed to protect her family and the village, she'd always found the place creepy. It was as though silently standing among them were a thousand ghosts watching her, waiting for her to join them. She didn't believe in ancient curses or vampires; she wasn't even sure she believed in an afterlife, but something had drawn her here to say goodbye to her father in the spot on which he'd died.

The earth beneath the blood stone had been replaced, but it was clear to see where it had been disturbed and she laid the bouquet of flowers on top. As she bent down, she heard a noise. It sounded like a voice coming from across the field behind. She didn't catch what the voice said, apart from one word which sounded like 'blood'. Had it been the rustle of her coat, a bird, or the sound of someone on the road a few hundred yards away?

Carole looked around her and realised she was isolated and alone. As the sun dipped below the waves, her heart began to beat faster. She should go and see how her mother was getting on. She was probably worried because she'd been gone a while.

The cold breeze was making her cheeks and chin cold; the type of wind that should it go up a few notches would give you a headache. However, it wasn't the wind which was giving her goosebumps and making the hairs on the back of her neck stand up. She was a grownup professional woman who didn't believe in stories and legends, so she forced herself to stand there a moment longer. Straining to hear the sounds around her. The wind was fresh off the sea, carrying only the scent of salt. Her ears heard no more voices, not even a bird or seagull. They'd settled in for the night. Satisfied that she'd proved herself immune to irrational fears, she decided it was time she went home too.

She walked across to her car, but couldn't help locking the doors behind her once inside. She also found herself checking the back seat. She was being silly. This wasn't like her to feel on edge, but she rationalised it as being the effects of grief. The sudden loss of a parent had shaken her world.

She'd have to negotiate the rough dirt track that led along the top of the cliff before she reached the main road. It was bumpy and so she'd need to take it very slowly, turning her headlights on full beam so she could spot any large rocks that might tear her tyre. She'd been stupid, coming here so late. It would have been far safer in daylight.

Before she turned her engine on, Carole took her mobile phone from her handbag and dialled her parents' home. It rang four times and was eventually picked up by the answerphone. She nearly ended the call, but she was worried her mother might be getting concerned and had simply been unable to reach the phone in time, so she spoke to the answerphone. Or was it that she needed the comfort of feeling like she was talking to someone and she wasn't totally alone out here?

'Hi mum, I'm just leaving the blood stone. I brought some flowers from us all for dad, but I'm heading back...'

Carole didn't finish her sentence. Coming through the bushes to the side and behind of her, was a hideous sight which made her heart leap into her throat.

'What the...'

It looked like a walking corpse, dressed in ragged clothing and with white skin, mottled with grey. Dark rings surrounded its eyes, and the nose was hooked and sharp with two large upper front teeth. It walked towards the blood stone and hadn't seemed to have noticed her black car off to the side in the darkness.

'Oh my God, there's somebody... something... it's like... a vampire!' Carole exclaimed.

As she stared, a group of around eight more figures appeared out of the shadows behind him. There were females in long dresses, and male figures in dinner suits.

'There's more of them.'

Was she hallucinating? Had grief brought on some strange psychological trauma?

She panicked. All rational thoughts had left her mind. The legends and stories told to her and passed down through the centuries, all collided in her head. All she wanted to do was get away.

Carole threw her phone onto the passenger seat and turned the engine on, all the while not taking her eyes away from the hideous group that had instantly turned their faces towards her at the sound of the car engine. She didn't wait any longer. She slammed her foot on the accelerator, wheels spinning on the gravelly track. Behind her, some of the group had moved towards her, hands outstretched. She wasn't going to wait and see what they wanted. She had to get away and to the safety of the main road.

Her heart was beating so fast she thought it would burst. What had she just seen?

She kept checking her rear-view and side mirrors, terrified that they might have followed her, be chasing her. Be about to bang on her windows and doors, trying to get in.

She'd forgotten her mobile was still connected to her mum's answerphone. Forgotten that the track was narrow and full of rocks. Forgotten her rational thinking. Forgotten the edge of the cliff was only a couple of feet from the dirt track. She was overcome with fear.

As her eyes once more flicked to the rear-view mirror, they returned to the track just in time to see a large, jagged rock loom out of the darkness. She swerved, panicking and intending to hit the brake to slow herself down, but her foot hit the accelerator instead and before she could do anything about it, she found her car wheels losing contact with the cliff top. It careered over the edge, plunging her into the darkness below. The curse had struck again.

2

Dr Harrison Lane walked out of Wandsworth police station into a new world. He'd been expecting them to accuse him of double murder, that hadn't phased him. What had, was just a few hours ago he'd been content in the knowledge that he'd never known who his father was, and never would. What he'd just heard in the interview room from Detective Inspector Gordon Jacobsen had rocked him to his core.

For a moment, he just stood and breathed. Breathing was underrated and under-appreciated by most people. Apart from the very obvious fact it's what keeps us alive, Harrison knew there were other physiological reasons why it could be used very effectively to calm and focus the mind.

His muscular chest rose and fell slowly underneath his jacket. Four counts in, hold the breath, and then eight counts out. Exhaling warmth into the chill December London air. It provided more oxygen to his brain and stimulated his vagus nerve and parasympathetic nervous system. These told his heart rate and blood pressure to lower, and his brain that it was time to be calm; the exact opposite of the stress reaction engendered by his sympathetic nervous system, the fight and flight response, which pumped blood to his muscles. By focusing on his breathing, he could calm the swirling thoughts in his head which were competing for his attention, and allow himself to think clearly and rationally.

There were a couple of reassuring things which he'd had confirmed during the conversation with DI Jacobsen. The first was his extreme gratitude that DS Jack Salter was such an organised and thorough detective, and that he's his friend. The second was the skill and dogged attitude of his assistant, Ryan, who could find anything or anyone online. They'd been busy while he'd been out of the UK in Jersey tracking down the mermaid killer, and managed to turn what could have been an extremely difficult situation into not much more than a 'strained' chat.

Harrison could see how it all looked, but as he was always so fond of saying, people look but they don't always see, and in this case, that was a definite.

Once he'd felt his heart rate slow and the tension dissipate in his muscles, Harrison lifted his dark head and looked at Wandsworth High street. His immediate concern was that all he wanted to do was head home to his Docklands apartment, where he could close the door and be alone with his thoughts. His Harley was parked at home so he would have to get the underground and Docklands light railway back. He hadn't taken much luggage on his trip to Jersey and so his bag wasn't too big and cumbersome. Weight wouldn't have been an issue for a man like Harrison, but bulk could be a pain on the crowded underground system. In all honesty, the last thing he wanted to do was be in a crowded enclosed space with hundreds of other people, but it was a means to an end.

Before he set off for the tube station, he pulled his phone from his pocket. It had been on silent but he'd felt it buzz several times during the last two hours. He replied to Tanya's message, thanking her for coming to the airport to warn him, and telling her he was fine. The situation was under control. Then he called Ryan.

'Boss!' His assistant picked up within one ring.

'I'm heading home. Everything's fine, thanks to you and Jack. I appreciate what you've done, Ryan.'

Harrison didn't wait for a reaction. He knew Ryan well enough to know that he'd be embarrassed by the gratitude, but he'd wanted him to know it all the same.

'Everything OK? Anything come in that needs my immediate attention?'

'Mostly small stuff. I've dealt with a couple of things, but there's a big case come up and they need you to head to Yorkshire. It's from the NCA. A weird one. It's in all the papers and all over social media.'

Harrison pictured Ryan sitting at his desk in their small basement office at New Scotland Yard, surrounded by his snacks and computer screens. They'd moved most of their stuff out, ready for their move to the National Crime Agency offices, their new work home. He wasn't going to miss the lack of natural light, but he would miss his quiet bolt hole hidden away from the hubbub of the rest of the police operations. He sighed.

'OK. Send it over.' Although he felt like he needed some time and space to process things, perhaps a new case was what he needed instead. Put some distance between himself and the last two hours and allow his brain to catch up with the latest revelation while he focused on something else.

'Jack wants you to call him,' Ryan added.

He'd been next on Harrison's list.

The conversation with Jack was short. He was at the scene of a road rage assault and couldn't talk. Harrison could hear the heated voices in the background. They arranged to meet later that evening for a catch up. Yorkshire could wait until the morning, Harrison wanted to spend at least one night in his own space.

His apartment, in a renovated tea warehouse, was like the land where time had stood still. Harrison had to leave for Jersey in a hurry and there'd been no time to clear away his breakfast bowl, or put the dishwasher on. He felt like he'd been away for months, so much in his life had changed in just a few days, but the flat looked and felt exactly as he'd left it. It was comforting.

He put the kettle on and made himself one of his favourite chamomile and limeflower teas, placing any dirty plates and mugs into the dishwasher and turning it on. It wasn't full, but the smell when he'd opened the door wasn't pleasant; the crockery that was already in there couldn't wait any longer. Then he'd sat down on the sofa in front of the huge glass windows which overlooked the Thames. He'd not been aware of just how tired he felt until that moment.

The pressure of dealing with the Mannings was emotionally exhausting. Since his mother's murder in 2004, he'd been harbouring the burning desire for revenge. Their evil had taken her away from him and very nearly destroyed him. It had only been the intervention of Joe, the man he called his stepfather, that had enabled him to turn that anger into a positive and forge the career path he now followed. The two girls in Jersey who had been spared the butchery of the psychopathic mermaid killer, were alive because of his mother. Every life he saved was because of her. For her. Every lie he could expose was to chip away at the lies which had called her murder a suicide, and to expose those who failed to investigate.

The Mannings, like so many others, preyed on people's beliefs and fears. The bread and butter of every religion and cult that had ever been created. Our human need to believe in something greater than the here and now, that life doesn't just end with a coffin and a headstone, and somehow our actions could have an impact on that outcome. Those beliefs could give hope in times of distress and trauma, but they could equally be used to destroy, torment, and discriminate.

Now though, he'd discovered a truth which he didn't want to believe. Ended a lifetime of not knowing with a scientific fact. He now knew who his father was. The man who had helped create him. The irony of his genealogy was overwhelming, and it opened up a whole new sink hole of questions and secrets which he could feel himself tipping into.

3

Harrison hadn't consciously fallen asleep, but he found himself being woken by his phone ringing. He'd probably not been out for long, but he'd surprised himself with the impromptu nap.

'Dr Harrison Lane?' The voice on the other end asked him.

'Yes.'

'I just wanted to make contact before you arrive. DI Adam Christie from Humberside.'

There was a pause while DI Christie waited for a reaction from Harrison. When there was none, he continued.

'Did you have any questions for me before you come up here? Anything you need us to be preparing?'

'I haven't read the full briefing yet,' Harrison replied. 'I've just got back from another case.'

'My apologies, and I know we're getting close to Christmas. You probably would far rather be at home with your family...'

Another pause.

'The Jersey case was a high profile one, the mermaid guy wasn't it? Good catch Dr Lane. Ours is less gruesome, but baffling. Three heart attacks and one over the cliff plunge, but it's got an entire village in a panic. We've whole families moving out after a young lad in his twenties died in his sleep. They think the curse has hit the family and is now coming down on the village.'

'The curse?'

'Yes, the Templeton family curse, that's what's being blamed for the deaths, but of course, we're looking for a rational explanation.'

'Apart from the curse, what other ritualistic elements are involved?' Harrison asked.

'The vampires. Perhaps you haven't seen the headlines. Carole Templeton, the one who plunged over the cliff. She seemingly drove off the edge while being chased by a pack of vampires. She was visiting the scene of the first death, her father's at a stone circle. One of them, the blood stone, was supposed to have a vampire buried beneath it in the 1700s and her father had been digging there. Now they think that because the ground was disturbed, it's been let loose.'

'How do you know what she saw? Did she survive the crash?'

'No. She was on the phone to her mother at the time, recording a message on the answerphone. Terrible thing for her mother to hear after she'd just lost her husband as well.'

'I'll be with you tomorrow morning,' Harrison replied.

'Right. Good. I look forward to meeting you. We'll be based out of a small local police station, but anything you need, just ask.'

Harrison slumped back on the sofa. It was pleasing to know that his reputation now ensured him a warm welcome in investigations like this. That certainly hadn't always been the case. The blood stone curse had intrigued him. He felt the familiar bubble of anticipation that always came when he started on a new mystery. His power nap had also given him some renewed energy. When things were preying on his mind, he usually did one of two things: either go for a run or meditate. As he'd been away and not had much chance to exercise, and may not over the next couple of days, he decided to go for a run.

The air was cold, slamming into his face and lungs with an icy slap, but he enjoyed its challenge. He wanted to be rid of the knots of tension that had settled into all his major muscles, making his body feel like a current of electricity had been coursing through it, spasming and contracting. Harrison had a few hours before he'd arranged to meet Jack, plenty of time to expend that negative energy and recover. He headed for the river, where he could run along its banks, his feet pounding rhythmically, running away from the spectre of his new found knowledge. It was like an image that he'd seen and wished he hadn't. He couldn't get it out of his head, no matter how hard he tried.

A lone female jogger was heading towards him. Her eyes focused on the big six feet two inches of muscular man in front of her, in the hope she might catch his eye. The dating apps were all well and good, but she'd far rather meet someone in their natural environment. When they were almost upon each other, she said 'Hi'.

Harrison gave a brief nod and swerved to give her a wide berth, always aware that some women might feel intimidated when out alone.

He missed the disappointment on her face as he powered past and left her deflated.

Another one who got away, she thought. There'd been no ring on his wedding finger. Shame.

Harrison was as usual, oblivious to it all. He had a remarkable talent for understanding people, being able to interpret their thoughts through their actions, until it came to females attracted to him. For some reason, he had a total blind spot in that regard.

Harrison ran on and on, his chest and muscles burning. When he turned round to head back home, he picked up the pace, pushing his body, and enjoying the pain. Now he had nothing in his head besides the screaming of his muscles and the rhythmic puffing of his breath, squeezing in and out of his body. His heart pumped hard in his chest as it attempted to get oxygenated blood to all the places that needed it. By the time he reached his flat, he was like a steaming race horse off the gallops. He did some stretches and then stripped off and into the shower.

Harrison's rippling tight abdominal muscles would have more than delighted the female jogger earlier, had she been lucky enough to see them. Unfortunately for her, he showered alone and then headed downstairs to his Harley Davidson. He'd missed riding his bike and the feel of the engine starting up beneath him was a therapy in itself. It was time to go and meet Jack.

THEY'D ARRANGED to go to the same pub they'd met at before, the Pig 'n' Whistle. He wasn't one for going out, in part because he never drank, but the steak pie and chips had been good when they'd last eaten there, and he was now ravenous after his run.

When Harrison entered, he scanned the tables for his blonde-haired friend and was surprised to see it wasn't just Jack sat waiting for him.

'Ryan!' He exclaimed, smiling but with an undercurrent of concern.

'Jack brought me,' Ryan explained, 'and I'm sticking to Diet Coke.'

Harrison laid a hand on his shoulder, reassuringly.

Ryan's agoraphobia and anxiety had got him into trouble with drugs and drink in the past. He also smiled at Jack. Ryan would never have gone out on his own and it was good for him to go somewhere different than his own flat and the office. Either Jack had worked out the problem, or Ryan had confided in him. Either way, they'd clearly built on their relationship while he'd been away, because Ryan hadn't really trusted anyone besides Harrison. They'd come a long way in a few months from when the pair of them couldn't stand the sight of each other.

'Just waiting on the third member of your back-up team,' Jack joked.

Harrison looked quizzically at him, but he didn't need to answer because Tanya walked through the door into the pub at that moment. Her face lit up as she saw him, and Harrison was aware of his own responding in much the same way.

'So, let's order drinks and food and then get down to business. We need a full report of what was said today.' Jack took the lead.

As Tanya reached Harrison, he stood back up and gave her a quick kiss. She not only looked amazing, but she smelt amazing too, and he had to fight the urge to repeat the kiss. At work she tied her long brunette hair back, but tonight it was down and hung softly, framing her blue eyes, which were curtained with thick long lashes. Her skin was soft and tight across a sculptured face. She looked at him, searching his own handsome features for some indication of how he was feeling.

'You alright?' She asked quietly, taking his hand.

'I'm fine.'

They both sat down, aware of their companions, and Tanya concentrated on the menu that Jack passed across to her.

Ryan looked from her to Harrison and smirked.

Harrison raised his eyebrow.

'Not looking at the menu?' Jack asked him, looking up from his.

'Nope. Steak pie for me, please,' Harrison replied.

'I'll have the fish and chips,' Ryan spoke up.

'Scampi for me,' Tanya added.

'Drinks?' Jack asked. 'Let me guess, Orange juice for you,' he nodded at Harrison, 'another Diet Coke for Ryan, and Tanya, maybe a sparkling water?'

She smiled at him.

'I didn't drive, so nope. I'll have a Pinot Grigio, please. You lot might not need a drink, but I sure do.'

'A woman after my own heart,' Jack said, 'but unfortunately I am driving, so it's a Diet Coke for me too.'

While Jack crossed to the bar, Harrison's mind was filled with the image of Tanya on the back of his bike, her arms wrapped around him as they headed back to either his flat or hers. Was that why she'd not driven?

The second that Jack was back in his seat and everyone had their drink, he asked Harrison to tell them what had happened in the interview that morning.

'They started at the beginning, wanting to know how I knew the Mannings and why I'd gone to visit Freda in the hospice. I told them the truth. Explained my childhood, living with the Mannings in Wales, and that I believed my mother's death hadn't been suicide but that Freda and Desmond Manning had been responsible. I said I'd gone to ask her questions, see if maybe as she was dying that she might come clean.'

'Did you mention Nunhead?'

'Not until he did. I wasn't sure what you'd told him.'

'He knows your father's DNA was on the knife, and that Freda gave us the knife.'

Harrison nodded.

'That was his main question. The fact I hadn't declared my father when I joined the Met, that I hadn't told anybody about him.'

'What did you say?' Tanya asked him, her face full of sympathy.

'Again, the truth. I said I never knew who my father was. My mother had never told me and his name isn't on my birth certificate.'

'What did he say to that?'

'He said he would have to report it, that there might be an internal investigation.' Harrison shrugged. 'Ultimately, I can't see what they'll do about it. His name isn't recorded and there's no connection between us.'

'What about Freda's death, the fire, and the other corpse?'

'They agreed that Freda's death looked like an act of mercy covered up and were also on to the fact that the other body wasn't Desmond. He thought he'd been clever dousing it in petrol and burning it, but they managed to extract some DNA from a tooth. It matched a man on the system, low grade criminal, an addict. Thanks to you being so efficient and getting the CCTV from my flats, they also think it was him who stole my bike helmet. He had a distinctive tattoo on his hand, apparently.'

'Brilliant, and Ryan tracked him to where Desmond was staying. So are they now after him for murder?'

Harrison raised his eyebrow and nodded. 'They get that Desmond was trying to frame me and disappear.'

'Result!' Ryan exclaimed triumphantly.

'Yeah, but they've got to find him first. They wanted to know if I would have any idea where he might have gone.'

'I'll find him,' Ryan said, a steely determination in his eyes.

'He could have left the country by now,' Jack said despondently.

'I don't think so, not Desmond. He wasn't a man who liked to travel.' Harrison thought back to their time in Wales, when Desmond had been unable to understand why he missed living in America.

'You know they're going to have to interview your father about Nunhead?' Jack said tentatively. 'We'll have to pass it on to another team. Get a cold case investigation properly started for Annette Ward's murder.'

Harrison shrugged.

'It's good that Annette's family might finally see some justice. But you all keep calling him my father. He's not. He's never been any kind of a father to me and I have no idea what the relationship with my mother was like.'

All three of his friends fell silent around the table. He was the psychologist. He knew it wasn't that simple, but right now, he wasn't going to think about it.

Jack changed the subject.

'So, is Gordon, DI Jacobsen, done with you? Or do you think he still has questions?'

'I think he's done with me, at least as far as I'm aware. I can understand why he wanted to talk to me, he needed to understand my relationship with the Mannings, and when the DNA link showed up for my...' Harrison hesitated, 'biological father, well that would have rung any decent detective's alarm bells. But it's thanks to you all that they knew without a doubt that I wasn't responsible for the fire and the bodies,' Harrison said.

All three smiled back at him, and Harrison thought back to what DI Adam Christie had said to him on the phone earlier. His comment about not wanting to go away and leave his family at Christmas time. He might not have parents, siblings, or his own wife and kids, but there was more than one type of family.

4

After they'd eaten, they chatted for a while. Jack was looking forward to Christmas with his wife Marie and their son, Daniel.

'It will be Daniel's first Christmas,' he'd said, beaming at them all. 'I know he won't remember it, or be aware of Father Christmas and all that, but I'm so looking forward to it. Marie is even thinking about us going to the kids' Christmas Eve service.' He threw a glance at Harrison.

'You know that Christmas time was almost definitely not when Jesus was born?' Harrison took the bait. 'They chose the date because it coincided with the winter solstice, which was already being celebrated by the pagans, and they wanted to supersede it. There's no birth date for him in the bible. He was probably born in June, which would fit with the lambs and the rest of the evidence.'

'Thanks doctor doom, and I suppose next you're going to tell us that Father Christmas isn't real either?' Jack smirked at him.

Harrison raised an eyebrow.

'He was probably based on a real man who was given

saintly status, St Nicholas, but I think you know that our modern variant is a relatively new commercial phenomenon.'

'Well, before you entirely trash the Christmas spirit, I'd better get Ryan home,' Jack replied. He said it tongue-in-cheek, and Harrison knew Jack was also playing cupid because he thought he and Tanya might like some time alone. They'd not seen each other for days, apart from the brief meeting at the airport, and he'd already told them all that he was off for Yorkshire the next day. No one around the table had missed the disappointment on Tanya's face when he said that.

Ryan had happily acquiesced to Jack's suggestion. Harrison could see that the initial euphoria of being out and in a pub had worn off, and Ryan was starting to get anxious. Harrison insisted on getting the bill. It was the least he could do to thank them for their help.

'I've missed you, despite your overly practical view of our beloved holiday season,' Tanya said to him, smiling, after they'd gone, moving from the chair where she'd been sitting in the group to come and sit closer to him.

'Me too,' he'd replied, losing himself in her eyes for a few moments and ignoring her other comment. 'I'm sorry I have to go away again tomorrow. You know this is what it's going to be like. I'll be travelling all over the country with the NCA, so are you sure you want to continue like this?'

Tanya's eyes scanned his face for a few moments, and then she smiled.

'I'm sure. I'd rather have you once a week than not at all.'

'And what about my so-called father? How do you feel knowing that I come from someone like him?' Harrison surprised himself with the lip snarl that accompanied his words. Had it made him feel differently about himself? Would it make Tanya feel differently about him?

'As you said, he's never been your father. It changes nothing.' She placed both her hands around his and he felt the wave of anger, or maybe disgust, that had shot through him, disappear.

'Perhaps we should get you home too?' He suggested.

'I thought maybe you'd like to spend a night in your own bed,' Tanya replied and then added teasingly, 'I've brought my toothbrush.'

WAKING up next to Tanya started his morning full of warmth, despite the dull, cold, grey winter's day outside. He lay next to her, just watching her sleep for a few minutes, until her eyelids flickered and she smiled her good morning.

'You OK?' She asked, wrapping her limbs around his and lying her head on his big chest.

'Fine. It's just nice to have you here.'

'Do you remember the nightmare?'

'Nightmare?' Harrison scowled, thinking hard. 'No.'

'You woke me up about three am. I thought you were going to kick me out of bed at one point. I don't know who you were fighting, but I think you got the upper hand.' Tanya smiled.

Harrison quickly rolled onto his side and lifted up onto his elbow to look at her again, his face showing the concern he felt.

'I didn't hurt you, did I? Are you OK?' He reached out and stroked her cheek.

'I'm fine, I had to wake you up though. We spoke briefly. That's why I thought you might remember it.'

He shook his head. He knew that normal dreaming took

place in REM sleep when the muscles of our bodies are paralysed and only the rapid eye movement gives away our dreaming state. For him to have been acting out his dream physically, indicated a sleep behaviour disorder, probably brought on by the trauma of the previous day. It's during REM sleep that our brain processes our emotions, and in people who have post-traumatic stress disorders, this can go wrong and the negative emotions are over-consolidated and reinforced. His dream, or nightmare, was evidence of the inner turmoil he was trying hard to keep under control. He wouldn't have forgiven himself if he'd hurt Tanya. It was probably a good thing he was going away for a few days. Hopefully, by the time he got back it would have worked through and he'd be on top of his emotions.

That doubt crept back in again. The anger he sometimes struggled to control, his subconscious coming out in his dream. Were they signs that he was indeed his father's son?

'I'd better get in the shower,' Tanya's voice cut through his thoughts. 'We both need to head to work.'

He watched as she unwillingly slipped out of bed and padded across the bedroom carpet to the bathroom, naked and beautiful. He could have quite happily dragged her back and stayed in bed all day, but duty called.

While Tanya showered, Harrison went into the open plan living area and made them both tea. He stood nursing his mug and staring out of the window at the brown Thames waters, which never failed to keep on flowing past his flat. He'd always felt so lucky to be able to live in this apartment, courtesy of his grandfather's shrewd investment, even if London wasn't his ideal location for a home. The thought of him led Harrison to search out his mother's photograph on the coffee table. A beautiful young woman, frozen forever in a carefree smile. Why did she never resume contact with her parents? Why and how had she met his father? He had no idea of the nature of their relationship. All he knew was that as a child, he'd never felt deprived of love. Had she simply been naïve and manipulated? Or had she been truly in love with his father, flaws and all?

He realised that he didn't really know the woman who was his mother, her hopes and dreams, her failings and fears. She'd been his rock, the one constant in his life until that day she was taken away from him. After that, he elevated her to sainthood and nothing she'd done had been wrong. Perhaps he'd been blinded by her. Her contagious personality that sucked you in and made you want to be in her presence. But she was only human and humans make mistakes. What had hers been?

5

Reverend Brian Davenport didn't need to go and stand in his pulpit to know that his congregation had swelled. He could hear them from the vestry, the loud whisper of gathered people greeting each other, but not daring to speak full volume for fear of disgracing themselves or dishonouring God. That's the way it should be. A healthy respect for his Lord.

They had come to him today out of fear, seeking the refuge and protection of the church from the curse which they thought the blood stone had unleashed. He would give them the full fire and brimstone sermon performance today, show them who was in charge. The happy clappy modernists couldn't help people like them. What use would their fluffy prayers be in the face of real evil?

Most of them had abandoned him before now. Left his ministry for an allegiance with temptation, turned their backs on the gospel and instead exalted the plethora of worthless celebrities who preached their sinful heresies on social media. The Diocese had suggested he changed his style, softened and modernised his approach. They'd sent him on courses to help him diversify his thinking and become a more inclusive community leader. Their attempts had fallen on stony ground. He remained resolute in his belief and the sanctity of the rituals and traditions he undertook. Finally, they'd suggested it was time for him to retire, his church congregation was dwindling and the cost of keeping him on was simply not economical. When did worshipping his God become a decision on a balance sheet?

Now, though, neither he nor they could abandon his flock. The national media attention alone would ensure the Diocese kept his doors open, at least for now. He would be inside, piously waiting for those whose souls were troubled, or who had lost their way. He would also be waiting for Margaret Templeton, who had sought his comfort this week after the death of her husband and children. She was a fine woman with a fine house and no husband. He was a respectable man to whom she had turned for comfort and guidance. He wasn't a fool. Brian Davenport realised that the Diocese would ensure his tenure wasn't prolonged and he'd be out on his ear. With a wealthy widow as his sponsor and partner, then the future could be much brighter. He'd be able to continue his vocation of serving his Lord in comfort.

Reverend Davenport brushed a thread of loose cotton from his robe and prepared himself to meet his enlarged flock. He breathed in the comforting aroma of slightly damp stone and dust that had been his divine accompaniment for over two decades, and he sighed in satisfaction at his lot.

6

Detective Inspector Adam Christie awaited the arrival of Dr Harrison Lane with trepidation. He'd worked some tough murder cases before. At times he'd failed in his public duty and in his promise to the victim, of bringing their killer to justice, but there hadn't been a case where he'd simply not had a clue. Until now.

He wasn't even sure if murder had taken place, but he was pretty certain of it. After years of doing the job, you felt it in your gut. You don't get that many suspicious sudden deaths in one place and in such a short time frame, without there being some kind of third-party involvement. Problem was, if there was a killer, then they were more elusive than the invisible man.

Harrison Lane's reputation had drifted down from London on the police grapevine, and he'd been ecstatic when the National Crime Agency had said they'd send in the head of the Ritualistic Behavioural Crime unit. The appearance of vampires, a family curse, and religious hysteria had pushed Adam Christie way out of his comfort zone. When reception called to say Dr Lane had arrived, he sprung up out of his chair and headed down to greet the man he hoped would be their saviour.

Like so many before him, Christie's first impressions were not what he'd been expecting. Although Dr Lane came with a 'bit of a maverick' reputation, being confronted by over six feet of solid muscle in black bike leathers was on the further extreme of his expectations. He didn't care about what he looked like, though, just that he could do his job.

'Dr Lane, a pleasure to meet you. DI Adam Christie.' He'd extended his hand in greeting, bracing himself for a firm handshake. He got it. 'Come on upstairs and meet the team. Did Rosemary give you your pass?'

He looked at the receptionist and back at Harrison, who pulled a fob out of his pocket.

'Good, we're on the first floor. Everyone's expecting you.'

By the time they reached the office, DI Christie had already surmised that Dr Harrison Lane was a man of few words. That didn't bother him. It was the quality of his words, not the quantity he was interested in.

'OK everyone, I'd like to introduce you to Dr Harrison Lane, head of the Ritualistic Behavioural Crime unit. Dr Lane was working under the Met's command, but is now with the National Crime Agency, who have loaned us his services to see if we can get to the bottom of our series of unexplained deaths.'

Harrison nodded at the various officers and civilian personnel in front of him.

DI Christie continued.

'To my left we have DC Lucy Robinson. Next to her is Sergeant John Cutter, and this is DS Scott Haynes, with Andy Nesbitt as tech support.'

Harrison scanned the faces of the welcoming party. Lucy looked to be mid to late twenties, with one of those young faces that made it harder to tell age. She wasn't a fan of make-up, which might have made her appear younger, and Harrison noted the engagement ring on her left hand. She was, however, a cat lover, as evidenced by the hairs on her lower trouser legs, and it wasn't difficult to spot which desk she usually sat at because various cat paraphernalia adorned it.

Sergeant John Cutter was a man nearing retirement age, as too was DS Haynes. That seemed to be where similarities ended, however, as John Cutter appeared to be a rough, tough Yorkshire man who would be equally at home on a farm or out on the moors, whereas DS Haynes was cut from a different cloth altogether. He was impeccably turned out with a soft belly and soft hands, and the look of a man who believed he lived his life in a disciplined and righteous manner.

Andy Nesbitt was about Harrison's age, mid to late thirties, but had the misfortune to have the hair loss gene, which meant he was already thinning on top, but otherwise looked fit. Harrison guessed he was a cyclist from his physique, strong thighs, and the cycle helmet on one of the desks, which didn't look like it belonged to any of the other team members.

'Let's go and have a full briefing, let you know where we're up to with this, and then DS Haynes is going to take you to the various potential crime scenes. You're aware that we've no evidence that a crime has been committed in any of these cases, but they're all too coincidental to not be connected.'

Harrison looked at the DI. 'As humans, we try to connect things and make a pattern where there are random occurrences. It's possible that these cases are not connected at all,' Harrison said to him.

'Yes. Maybe. But there are strange circumstances surrounding each one and three are the same family, with the fourth connected to them. We do have a potential suspect and motive, but as to methodology, that's where I'm stuck. Then there are the vampires. A rational woman who didn't believe in the curse or anything supernatural like that dies after saying she has seen vampires.'

'Grief can cause immense mental stress. Suggestion on top of an already imbalanced mind through great emotional turmoil could account for hallucinations.'

'She sounded quite rational up to that point to me. I'll play you the voice recording.' DI Christie replied. 'Come this way, I've booked the meeting room and we have croissants and coffee coming.'

Harrison was shown into a standard issue police meeting room where a board with the various victim's faces on it, stood at one end. It was the kind of briefing room he was used to, but the addition of croissants was a welcome change. Five of them sat down, while Adam Christie went to stand next to the board.

'The first death was Richard Templeton, sixty-four years of age, seemingly a straightforward heart attack while digging, but Richard was a fit man. He regularly gardened. There'd been no reported issues with his heart, and the autopsy showed nothing untoward. Indeed, an eyewitness saw him approximately ten minutes before his estimated time of death, and he said he was looking well, waved and smiled at him, and showed no signs of being in distress.'

Harrison had read the autopsy report. Richard's heart and all its valves and blood vessels had indeed appeared to be healthy. The pathologist said it could have been the heart of a younger man. However, that didn't rule out an arrhythmia issue.

'Were the family questioned about any potential arrhythmia symptoms?' Harrison asked DI Christie.

'Yes. We have explained to them that there's no way to tell if a defect such as arrhythmia could have interrupted his heart, however his wife said he'd never told her he had irregular heartbeats, or appeared out of breath. He actually underwent some tests just a couple of years ago for his life insurance, and nothing had been shown up then either. Obviously, as a precaution, we instructed them all to consult a doctor and get tested.'

Harrison nodded.

'So, apart from the fact that it was a sudden and unexpected heart attack, which we know can happen, the other point of interest is the location and what he was doing. Richard was digging around and underneath the blood stone. Under the stone, legend has it, is a vampire who had terrorised the village in the seventeenth century, until he'd been staked, beheaded and buried under the stone to stop him rising. These stones are ancient, said to protect the people who live on the land around. They clearly didn't protect Richard Templeton, but he appeared to have been attempting to dig up something his grandfather had buried there. Henry Templeton had, so legend again would have it, returned from a trip abroad cursed by some ancient Malaysian deity, because he and two men from the village stole treasure from a temple. The two villagers never made it home alive. In order to stop the curse, Henry had buried whatever it was he took under the blood stone. Nobody had ever dared investigate what it was until Richard.'

'Really? There's supposed to be treasure buried there and nobody had tried to dig it up?' Harrison was surprised.

'Let's put it this way, not that we know of. The villagers

appear genuinely to believe the legend and weren't keen to tempt fate.'

'What did Richard find before his death?'

'All he'd uncovered was what appears to be some old spear and arrow heads wrapped in a leather cloth. Certainly none of the treasure he'd been hoping for.'

'Why now? Why dig there now?'

'They have money troubles. A big house with a small income, and lots of bills.'

'The house sustained damage in the storms last winter. Roof needs some serious repairs,' DS Haynes spoke up now, looking at Harrison.

'We return to the blood stone for death number two.' Christie continued. 'Carole Templeton, Richard's daughter, thirty-one and a successful lawyer in London, rising up through the ranks. Not married, but critically she had undergone a health screening recently as part of her work health insurance, and there was no evidence of any irregularities with her heart, or anything else. She was fit and healthy. Carole also didn't believe in any of the legends. She went to the blood stone in order to pay her respects to her father where he'd died. I'm going to play the recorded message left on her parents' answerphone.'

DI Christie pressed some keys on the laptop which sat on the table in front of him, and a woman's voice came on. She sounded calm and there was an element of forced cheerfulness in her voice, nothing that you wouldn't expect with family members recovering from a recent bereavement and trying to rally their spirits.

'Hi mum, I'm just leaving the blood stone. I brought some flowers from us all for dad, but I'm heading back...'

She didn't finish her sentence. There was a pause then, 'What the...'

Harrison could hear her breathing get faster. Something had frightened her at this point. He could almost see her blood pressure rising, her heartbeat quickening, and her body go into flight and fight mode.

'Oh my God, there's somebody... something... it's like... a vampire!' She exclaimed. Her voice had risen an octave as her throat tightened with fear.

'There's more of them.'

Then there was a scraping thud and the sound of the engine being turned on. This was quickly followed by the accelerator being floored and they could hear the wheels spinning for traction on the gravel before the sound of travelling over bumpy ground.

Carole swore, 'I can't believe... They're coming after me...'

There were a couple of scrapes and bangs which sounded like rocks on the underside of the car. Then Carole swore again, and the engine revved just as she screamed. The last thing on the recording was the sickening crunch of the car as it hit the rocks below.

'As I'm sure you'll appreciate, this was incredibly upsetting for her mother, who'd only just started mourning her husband. From our point of view, we have no idea what went on. We've contacted local theatre groups, put out a public request for information, and nobody has come forward.'

'Any known vampires around here?' Harrison asked.

'Known vampires?' DI Christie looked confused.

'Yes, there are some people who are haematomaniacs. They have a serious craving for fresh blood and actually seek consenting donors. They might identify as Sanguinarians and often have a small subculture of their own. I don't mean they live in coffins, have fangs and kill their victims. They're seemingly ordinary people with what they believe to be a medical condition that requires blood drinking. Then there are also others who just glorify the pop culture aspects of vampires, or are part of the extreme goth movement and might just have psychiatric issues.'

DI Christie's open mouth answered the question for Harrison.

'OK, I'll look into it,' he said to him reassuringly.

'Are you seriously telling us that there are real vampires out there?' Haynes spoke now.

'There are people who identify as blood drinkers, yes, but not in the way that vampires have been portrayed in films and books.'

'That's just plain sick and evil.' His voice was slightly raised, passionate.

Harrison decided to ignore the emotional outburst. He'd learned long ago not to get into a debate with someone who was arguing on an emotional level. He preferred facts to opinion.

'And the third death?' He turned and addressed DI Christie.

'Carole's brother, Jasper. Found dead three days after Carole's accident, a week after his father's death. Poor Margaret Templeton found him dead in bed. It was again deemed a heart attack, or heart failure, but with no obvious cause.'

'Had he been to the blood stone, or touched anything that had come from it?'

'No. There was a level of hysteria beginning to circulate that Richard had released the curse, but Jasper never went to the stones. He hadn't even left the house. He was staying with his mother. Usually lives in Peterborough with his wife and son. She's refused to visit now with their son, terrified that something might be going on with the family.'

'Again any history of heart disease?'

'No known history. His wife's getting their son checked out though, as a matter of urgency. Jasper had booked in for a test following advice, but it was for a couple of weeks' time, after his father's funeral.'

'And Margaret Templeton?'

'What do you mean?'

'Is she being tested? Heart arrhythmia can be inherited from the mother or father.'

'We have advised it, but the poor woman has just lost virtually her entire family and isn't really thinking rationally, or about herself right now.'

'And the fourth death?'

'Another heart failure. Young lad in the village. Totally out of the blue. Again died in bed.'

'What links does he have to the Templetons?'

'His family had worked for them in previous generations, much like a good deal of the village, but he wasn't directly linked. Recently graduated from University and just started in accountancy. His father is, however, the man we had down as a potential suspect in Richard's death. He'd been seen arguing with Richard the day before he died. Wanted to buy the house and lands from them. Richard refused.'

'That doesn't make sense then.'

'No. We still have him on the list of potential suspects. He's a doctor, you see, could have means, but when his son died, that confused matters. Now we have an entire village worrying they are going to die in their sleep. Some families have already moved out.'

'Apart from Carole, most of the deaths have been heart

failure. I'm presuming toxicology reports are back for all three?'

'For Richard and Jasper, yes. We're just waiting on Lee Rowland's results, the fourth victim.'

'All four victims' bodies still available?'

'Yes. Margaret Templeton isn't in any fit state to arrange a funeral anyway, and with the suspicions we have, we've requested that the coroner doesn't release them to the families yet.'

'Was Carole tested for any potential hallucinants?'

'They did the regular tests. Nothing. We'll get you all the witness statements and then DS Haynes will take you to the stones, and if Mrs Templeton is up to it, to the house.'

Harrison nodded thoughtfully. He was still not convinced that all the deaths were linked, or that foul play had taken place, but there was definitely a need to investigate. It could be someone clever using a natural cardiac or respiratory arresting poison, which was hard to detect and rarely found in standard pathology tests. He wanted to read all the witness statements, see if he could read between the lines and find anything that might explain what was going on. First, though, he wanted to visit the blood stone and get a feel for the place.

7

'It's ungodly what's been going on around here,' DS Haynes declared to Harrison, the minute they were in his car heading to the blood stone. 'Don't you agree?'

'I'm not sure what you mean by ungodly. There are a number of deaths, which may or may not be connected. They are either tragic coincidences that could have happened at any time, or they are the work of an evil human being, or potentially human beings. There will be rational explanations behind each, including what Carole Templeton saw.'

'A rational explanation for seeing vampires? Earlier you said that there are real vampires, people who drink blood. Don't you think that's ungodly?'

'DS Haynes, I do not subscribe to your categorisation of psychological or physical behaviours as ungodly or not. I view all cases from a scientific standpoint and try to avoid emotional responses to crime.'

'Emotional? You think I'm being emotional?'

'I think your view is your own. It is a view or

interpretation of the world that you adhere to. It is not one that myself or others might agree with. We all have our own belief systems, DS Haynes. Mine is based on looking at facts. I believe it is important to view the evidence we have before us with a totally impartial mind and not to colour the facts with preconceived perceptions.'

There was a cold silence in the car after that. Harrison was aware he'd rubbed the DS up the wrong way with his short lecture, but he wasn't bothered by that. He was here to do a job and not to massage the ego and religious conflicts of a detective. If Haynes came at this investigation with a set viewpoint, then that would totally colour everything he saw. How could anyone find out the truth if certain presumptions and suppositions had already been made?

They drove the rest of the way to the blood stone in silence. When they finally arrived, Harrison could tell Haynes had to make a big effort to talk to him professionally.

'There's a car park here, and then we can walk across the field to the stones.'

'Where was Carole Templeton parked if she managed to go off the cliff?'

'She drove up the track that leads directly to the stones. It's rocky, so I'd rather not go that way. She had a 4 by 4. But we can walk along and I'll show you where she went over.'

Harrison got out of the car and looked around. There were plenty of tyre marks for him to see, but clearly no way to be able to tell when they'd been put there. He was several days too late for tracking anything. He just needed to get a feel for the place, see what was possible.

Harrison followed Haynes, who was striding ahead of him along a worn dirt track through what was a rough field, dotted with gorse bushes. It was land that was only suitable for sheep grazing. He was interested in seeing if it was possible to hear a car arrive in the car park when you were standing at the stones. As he walked, he was aware that they were walking up a slight incline. While he could hear the sea in the distance, it was as they crested the top of the field and were greeted by the sight of a flat area of land that the full sound of the waves hit his ears. It had the effect of being like an infinity pool, an area of land that was a few hundred metres in depth, that just seemed to end where the sea began. Most spectacular were the huge granite stones which stood in a rough circle like watchmen looking out to sea. Against the sun, the stones were dark and impenetrable, sinister and other worldly; as he got closer, their surface seemed to come alive. Thousands of crystals glinted and shone across their surface, reflecting the sky and all around them.

'This one's the blood stone.' DS Haynes tipped his head at the largest stone. It stood at the head of the group, closest to the sea, around twenty metres from its nearest companion.

Harrison walked up to it, noticing the bouquet of flowers at its base; the blooms wilted and drying. The ground around it had clearly been dug over fairly recently, it was clear of all grasses and sea heather. He stood and scanned the whole area. In front was nothing but sea and sky. He could understand why ancient people had chosen this spot to worship their gods of nature. There was a clear line of sight to watch the sun rise in the east and set in the west, the arc of light that would travel across the sky giving life and warmth. At night, the sky would be filled with stars and the moon, reflected in the dark waters, which would give away their true nature by sending the reflections skipping and bouncing along its surface as the waves rolled and broke.

When he looked behind him, the way they had come was hidden below the brow of the incline. It meant that somebody could park and walk across the field of gorse to the stones, without being seen. The roaring of the sea also ensured you wouldn't hear a vehicle arriving in the car park. This was an isolated spot. One that people had once deemed sacred, and it still carried an air of sanctity around it.

'This place gives me the creeps,' DS Haynes broke into his thoughts. 'Feels like you're being watched all the time.'

For once, Harrison could empathise with the statement.

'It's the stones, tricking the mind. Our peripheral vision can see them standing around us so it confuses our brain, makes it think that there are people standing behind us. That engages our primitive fight and flight responses that warn us if potential danger is near. We know they're there, we know they're stones, but our brain receives conflicting information, which gives us the unsettled feeling.' Harrison said to him. He was rewarded with a humph from the DS.

Despite the feeling of being watched, the place felt totally at one with nature, out on a rocky limb above the sea and below the sky. Harrison looked to his right where the cliff edge curved inwards and a rocky dirt track could be seen following its course. The dirt track was just a few feet from the edge. Harrison started to walk along it.

'Any idea where Carole was parked? Where she started her phone call?'

The DS, who seemed to have been appeased by Harrison's explanation of being watched, walked up alongside him.

'We think she was parked just along here. We found skid marks from her tyres heading off from that point.'

Harrison looked to the ground. From the position Haynes had shown him, there was indeed clear evidence of small stones having been disturbed. The wind would have long ago rubbed out any tracks on the dusty ground, but as he walked he saw occasional gouges and disturbed earth, although it could have come from other vehicles, no doubt the emergency services who arrived later. The DS didn't need to point out the area that she went off the cliff. The bushes and plants were damaged and an area was flattened where her rescuers would have tried to reach her from the top. Harrison stopped on the track and looked behind him. The stones were still just visible. The memory of the fear in her voice on the answerphone, her words, 'they're coming after me,' echoed in his head. If people had arrived at the stones, she'd still be able to see them, but why would they have gone after her if they were innocent, unless the atmosphere of the place had got to her already fragile mind and she was mistaken? She had seemed very certain, though.

'What time was it when she went over?'

'Just around 4pm.'

'So the sun had likely set, or at least virtually gone. It would be almost dark.'

'Yes, and the cloud cover meant we had no moonlight that night.'

'So she could easily have been mistaken about what she saw?'

'She seemed pretty certain in her description that they were vampires.'

'The location would have planted the thought of vampires in her mind. In near darkness, and with a fragile emotional state from having come here to remember her father's recent death at this spot, she could have misinterpreted what she saw.'

'We've run a media campaign asking for anyone who might know what happened to come forward, anyone who was in the area, but we've had nothing.'

'Any possibility of being able to track vehicles which might have been in this area?'

DS Haynes shook his head.

'No, too remote. We've got no cctv for miles, private or public, and again, no witnesses who reported seeing any vehicles.'

Harrison walked closer to the edge and looked down. There was nothing but rocks and sea.

'She'd have died instantly. Hadn't even put her seat belt on, so the pathologist said the head injury she received would have taken her out immediately. The state of the car means there's no way of knowing how she came to go over. It could have been she was going too fast and lost control, or that she swerved to avoid something.'

Harrison stood a moment, playing through her answerphone message in his head. She'd seemed perfectly calm as she started the call. Would have planned to put on her seatbelt and start the car after she'd finished leaving the message, only what she saw interrupted her. Despite her initial calm state, what she saw, or thought she saw, had terrorised her enough for her to somehow career over the edge of the cliff to her death. There had to be somebody here with her, several people. So why hadn't they come forward?

'Who called the emergency services?'

'Her mother. Picked up the answerphone message immediately and rang it in.'

'So the people, our so-called vampires, didn't call it in?'

'No. That's odd, don't you think? Most people would dial 999 unless they had come to scare her and kill her on purpose.'

'Not if they were innocent and thought they'd be blamed. Maybe that's why they're not coming forward. Carole saw something that evening. We've just got to figure out what and who and why they were here.'

8

Ryan took a moment to study a particularly large cheese and onion crisp. He marvelled at the fact it was around three times bigger than all the other crisps in the packet and yet had somehow made it through production, transportation, the retailer, and to his desk, without being broken. Here it was, the lucky one, the one that had survived against the odds, and now it was about to be shattered into a hundred pieces and crunched in his mouth. He felt blessed that he had been chosen to take its perfect form and consume it. He opened his mouth as wide as he could and slotted the crisp inside, being careful that it didn't bite back and cut into his gum. He closed his mouth down on it and tasted the joy of cheese and onion on his tongue, followed by the satisfying natural potato flavour. Heaven.

Ryan was tired after his trip out to the pub with Jack and Harrison. The emotional strain of battling his agoraphobia had been tiring in itself, but it had also left him wired and unable to sleep, so he'd not had a good night's rest. There was also an element of relief from finding out that Harrison wasn't going to be framed and charged with murder. His boss was his rock, he owed him his life and his freedom and there was no one else in the world who'd ever taken the time to help him like Harrison.

He had to admit that lately he'd been surprised by Jack. When he'd first met him he was a loud, annoying idiot, but he'd proven himself to be a good friend to Harrison and any friend of his was a friend of Ryan's. He now had two people he could call friends.

That's not to say he didn't like Tanya too, but Ryan's experience of women was limited and he still saw them as being like some kind of separate race that he couldn't quite understand. He'd had a girlfriend when he was seventeen. They'd met in the therapy group his school had put him forward for. Life had been tough then, but at least as an under 18-year-old, he'd received some support. Molly also suffered from anxiety and agoraphobia. They found themselves to be kindred spirits for around a year, until her parents took her out of the group and she moved away. Ryan still kept in touch with her on social media, but it was infrequent contact now. The couple of years when he'd spiralled down after hitting adulthood and finding himself alone had pulled them apart.

There had been a few new emails when he got into the office. A couple were fairly straightforward requests for identification of symbols found at crime scenes. They had a bank of these which Ryan had built a searchable database for, and so he was able to quickly identify the ones they'd received that morning and supply some background information on them. This was the first step for cases like these which didn't involve murder, serious injury or crimes against children. If what he told the investigating officers, then threw up more questions, it would get passed on to

Harrison for review. More often than not, it was teenagers trying to be clever or throw the police off their scent, or those with drug addictions, off their heads. Harrison had added private notes to each of the symbols, which gave them a rough severity rating. Ryan knew that if certain ones came up, he was to flag it with Harrison. This morning's crop were thankfully all minor, his boss had enough on his plate without adding more work.

Since they'd learned who Harrison's biological father was, Ryan had done some reading up on him. He felt a little like he was betraying his confidence at first, snooping behind his back, but he figured that it could actually be useful if he knew a bit about him. There was no telling when something might crop up that this information could be useful for. If there was anything he'd learned while working with Harrison, it was that the past will almost invariably rear its head in the present, and being forewarned was forearmed.

There had been plenty about Harrison's father in the media, and once Ryan had separated the hype and sensationalism from the fact, it became more than clear that the two men bore no resemblance to each other, apart from each having an imposing physique. Ryan knew that Harrison's first question was how his mother had met him and what kind of relationship they'd had - if any. He started to do as much digging as he could, attempting to track his whereabouts and activity in the couple of years prior to Harrison's birth. It was difficult and slow progress, the guy hadn't exactly wanted to be monitored, but he wasn't about to give up. He wanted to be able to give his boss the answers he craved.

While working through that, Ryan was also attempting to track down Desmond Manning. The low life had made

Harrison's life a misery for years - not to mention his childhood and the potential murder of his mother - he wanted him arrested and put away for the crimes he'd committed. He knew exactly how he'd left London, and it was just a case of tracking his movements methodically to work out where the rat had gone to ground. On this, he was making good progress.

9

The Templetons' house wasn't a mansion, but it was a large country house set in its own grounds. It was clear that the estate had seen better days. The driveway was potholed and amateur attempts had been made to fill in holes with gravel, which would clearly only work as a temporary measure. There were no formal gardens as such. The lawns outside the front of the house were mown, but apart from the fields where sheep grazed, the rest had become one large pollinator patch, untended and left to nature.

From a distance, the house looked impressive. A stone statue of a rearing horse was directly in front of the entrance, allowing cars to circle around it. To the left, the gravel drive continued to some single-storey buildings that Harrison presumed might be garaging; a one time carriage house, home to the horses and the carriage they'd pulled.

In the gloomy winter light, the house gave the appearance of tired sadness, as though it too was somehow grieving with the family who inhabited it. A large patch on the roof showed where the damage had occurred last winter, and was now covered up temporarily like a giant band-aid.

As they drove closer, there didn't appear to be any life inside. All the windows reflected the grey sky. There was no evidence of the impending Christmas festivities. No light or colour. Life had come to a halt. The house was in mourning. Wrapped in aspic and frozen in time.

'The Templetons have been here for several generations. Henry Templeton built the house, owned most of the land around here, although nowadays they've sold off a fair bit of that. Made his money in iron ore, worth a fortune at one time, but that's slowly slipped away with each generation.' Haynes gave Harrison a short history lesson as they pulled up outside the house. 'No idea how they manage to afford to run this place nowadays, must cost an arm and a leg to heat and that's before all the maintenance. Can't see Margaret wanting to keep this on now.'

'Who lives or lived here full time?' Harrison asked.

'Just Margaret and Richard. Both their kids had grown up and moved away for work. They were active in village life, he played his part as squire when required.'

'She on her own here now?' Harrison asked, surprised and concerned.

'I believe that her sister has arrived from Ireland to be with her.'

Harrison sighed for the weight of grief he was about to be presented with. Losing your husband was bad enough, but to also lose both your children at the same time would be too much for many souls.

'I don't want her getting upset,' Haynes continued. 'She's been through a lot.'

'Do you know her?' Harrison asked, ignoring the obvious statement that had just been made.

'We go to the same church, the one in the village. I live out the other side, so know this area well.'

'If you don't mind, I'd like to speak to her alone,' Harrison replied.

DS Haynes's head spun round to look at him. Harrison could feel his eyes boring into his head.

'Alone? Without me? Absolutely not. I've no conflict of interest. We don't know each other that well.'

Harrison sighed again and turned slowly to look the detective in the eyes.

'I am a trained psychologist used to interviewing victims. I need to speak with Mrs Templeton without any potential interruptions or leading questions. I bring a fresh pair of eyes to this situation, whereas you have lived experience and knowledge which has a place in this enquiry, but not in this initial fact-finding phase. I am also an outsider, which presents no embarrassing conflicts with regard to how our relationship will progress after this enquiry. I won't be bumping into her in church, thus saving her from the embarrassment of knowing that I might be privy to sensitive private matters. I therefore respectfully request that you allow me to interview Mrs Templeton alone.'

'No. That's not on.'

'Then we need to speak to DI Christie and get his opinion, as it appears we have a stalemate,' Harrison calmly replied. He'd expected this might not be simple, but he wasn't going to budge. He watched the veins in Haynes's temple bulge and throb as he gritted his teeth. He already had a suspicion that there might be some animosity in that relationship, DS Haynes was around fifteen years further down the line in his career than Adam Christie, and yet he was a DS and Adam was DI. He was not going to want to be told to back down by him.

Harrison pulled his mobile phone from his pocket, ready to call his bluff.

'I'll agree to it this once, but only because I don't want to cause Mrs Templeton any embarrassment,' Haynes hissed at Harrison.

Harrison knew that was not the reason why, and he could have easily put the DS in his place, but he chose not to. Their relationship was already fractured, and they needed to work together on this case. He let it go.

'I'll come in and introduce you,' the detective added. 'I am allowed to express my condolences, I presume?' He added sarcastically.

'Of course,' Harrison replied without rising to the emotion.

The pair of them got out of the car and walked across the crunchy gravel towards the front door. The light battleship grey sky of earlier had darkened further to a solid gunmetal, and the first spattering of light rain splashed against their faces. The forecast hadn't been good; the weather was expected and if they were right, it would be continuing for the rest of the day. A spot of rain didn't bother Harrison, unless he was on his motorbike, so for once he was glad that he was being chauffeured around by Haynes, even if the man was an irritation.

The man in question rang an ancient doorbell, and even through the thick wooden front door, its tenor tone could be heard announcing their arrival to those inside. The pair of them stood silently. Harrison could see Haynes still bristling at having his authority challenged, but the second the door swung open, it was all change and a full charm offensive.

'Margaret, I'm so sorry that we're disturbing you at this terrible time. I'm here in my official capacity, I'm afraid, and this is Dr Harrison Lane, who is assisting with our enquiries.'

'Enquiries? What exactly are you investigating?'

The woman in front of them looked as though someone could knock her over with one finger. She was of average height and build, but to Harrison, she was like a leaf skeleton. The past week had sapped her of all her life force and the grief showed on her face and in her posture. She seemed to be hanging on to the open door frame for support.

'May we come in?' DS Haynes continued in what Harrison presumed was his most soothing voice, but which to him came across as somewhat condescending. The main thing was that Mrs Templeton was too upset to notice or care. She let go of the door and turned, walking into the entrance hall and leaving the door open. They took that as their invitation to enter.

Harrison could tell not just the style of a house but that of its owners, by the entrance hall. This one was elegant, definitely a statement hallway, but not too in your face. Its aim had obviously been to showcase to all visitors the money and taste that went into its production, but without making it seem pretentious. Harrison suspected that around its walls had once hung large portraits and paintings, but their absence today was probably more down to the family's financial situation than the fact they didn't like them.

As they followed Margaret Templeton through a doorway, another door was flung open down the end of the hall, and a very bouncy and excited cockapoo came skidding across the tiles towards them. Harrison smiled and immediately bent down to greet the dog, while Haynes quickly ducked into the room after their host.

'Who are you?' a woman's voice cut into his dog greeting.

Harrison looked up to see a woman who looked virtually identical to Margaret Templeton, bearing down on him. She definitely didn't look like she'd blow away in the wind. She was strong and fit and determination held her face muscles tight as she glowered at Harrison.

'Police,' he quickly moved to reassure her, aware that they were two women alone in the house. Her face relaxed slightly.

'You don't look like police,' she challenged, resuming her scowl. 'If you're a reporter...'

Harrison stood up straight and pulled his ID from his pocket.

'Dr Harrison Lane, Head of the Ritualistic Behavioural Crime unit.'

'What are you doing here? My sister has just lost her husband, daughter, and son. She's bereft and doesn't need any more stress. She's already given statements. What's going on?'

'I understand your protectiveness, Mrs ?..' He waited a moment for her to reply.

'Ciara, just call me Ciara.'

'Ciara, I have been requested to help with an investigation to confirm that your family's deaths are indeed accidental and natural. Your niece's phone message has obviously caused some concern.'

'You're not suggesting...'

'We're not definitely suggesting that anything untoward has gone on, but we owe it to the deceased to ensure that all possibilities have been investigated.'

Ciara's resolve wavered as the grief she too was clearly trying to hold in nearly broke the surface. She gave a brief nod and led the way through the doorway that the dog, DS Haynes, and her sister had already gone through.

The dog may have greeted Harrison warmly, but it knew who its mistress was, and that she was suffering. When they entered the sitting room, Mrs Templeton was sitting on a sofa that could easily fit two, if not three people. This was however, clearly not going to be an option because although the lady of the house resembled a shrunken child, curled into the corner of the cushions, the dog had taken up a guard position and had its head resting on her leg and its body stretched across the rest of the available space. Despite its apparent resting pose, it eyed Harrison warily as he approached its mistress, sending a clear signal that he wasn't to upset her.

Margaret Templeton barely acknowledged Harrison's arrival. He knew the shattered look of grief. Glassy eyes that stared unbelieving at the world which no longer included their loved one. In Margaret's case, she'd lost the entirety of her immediate family in just over a week, and she was clearly struggling to comprehend her new reality.

'Mrs Templeton, I'm very sorry for the loss of your husband and children,' Harrison began. 'I don't want to cause you any distress and I'll be as quick as possible, but we need to fully understand the circumstances surrounding their deaths.'

Margaret Templeton lifted her chin very slightly to acknowledge Harrison's words.

Mindful of the dog's need to do its job, Harrison sat across from them, leaving the chair next to the sofa to serve as a comfortable safety buffer. DS Haynes stood like a spare part, eyeing him more aggressively than the dog. Harrison gave him a long look.

'I'll go and put the kettle on, shall I?' He said reluctantly. 'Ciara, do you want to show me where to find the mugs and tea?'

'Well, I'm not sure if...'

'I'll be fine, Cee,' Margaret said to her sister, causing them all to turn and look at her, surprised that she'd spoken.

Ciara gave an almost imperceptible tip of her head in acknowledgement and, with one final warning glance at Harrison, left the room with Haynes.

'If you don't mind, let's start with your husband, Mrs Templeton. Would you talk me through how he came to decide to go to the stones that day?'

Margaret Templeton's face told him of her regret.

'Are you familiar with the story of Henry, Richard's grandfather? It was him who'd amassed the family fortune, but Arthur, Richard's father, was very good at spending it. Richard inherited this house and the land, but there was no cash or family business left. He spent his life struggling to keep this place going, but we're fighting a losing battle. The maintenance of a big old building like this one is never ending; then there's the land and the running costs. The roof was damaged in a storm last winter and the only way we can pay for the repairs is if we sell more farm land. If we do that, then our annual income goes down. It's a vicious circle.'

Harrison listened to the defeat in Margaret Templeton's voice and wondered if she would have the fight, or even the will, to keep the estate now her husband and children were gone.

'There had always been a rumour that Henry had buried some kind of treasure he'd brought back from Malaysia, but which he believed to be cursed. I think Richard decided that the risk of the curse was outweighed by the need to fix the roof and so he decided to investigate. The rest you know.'

Margaret seemed to deflate another notch as she

finished her story. Harrison gave her a moment and then asked his questions.

'Would you say he was particularly stressed prior to going?'

'Not really. We've lived with money issues all our married lives. He knew both the children had offered to help with the roof repairs, but he got a bee in his bonnet about the legend and couldn't let it rest.'

'Why now? He'd known about the legend all his life, so why did he choose this time to try to see if there was treasure?'

'It was a conversation he'd had with the Vicar and Bob Williams at the autumn fair. Bob's been researching the history of the village and our family. Richard found it a bit of a cheek that he was looking into the Templetons and planning on publishing a book. The Vicar was trying to save the church from closure, so he's been looking into the old legends and stories to create interest.'

'Was there a disagreement?'

Margaret paused a moment.

'It was a heated discussion and I think Richard took umbrage at some of the things that Bob suggested about his grandfather, but nothing more than that.'

'Do you know what it was that upset Richard?'

'No. He didn't want to discuss it, but I think their conversation got him thinking about the stories, that's all. I think he figured if it was about to be publicised, then he had better check it out first, but he didn't really discuss it with me before he went.'

'Was there anything else worrying him? Any other disagreements?'

'No. My husband wasn't a man who made enemies. He

would far rather keep the peace and avoid conflicts. He was a gentle man.'

'And you told the other officers that there were no indications he was ill or had a heart condition.'

'Absolutely none. He was fit and healthy. I don't understand how he could have had a heart attack. It doesn't make sense. He did a lot of the work on the grounds himself. Just that week he'd been chopping trees and digging one of the field ditches out. He was healthy. Hadn't seen a doctor in years.'

'Do you have any idea what could have happened? Did you speak to him while he was there?'

'He left just after lunch. I tried calling him when he didn't return home for dinner, but by then, I believe he'd gone.'

Margaret's voice broke and her hand reached for the dog's head on her lap, for comfort.

Harrison knew an afternoon dog walker had found Richard Templeton, stone cold dead, and the pathologist estimated time of death at around three pm.

'Did he believe in the curse?' Harrison asked her gently.

Margaret shook her head.

'I only wish he'd taken more heed of it.'

'Do you believe in it?'

She looked Harrison straight in the eyes.

'I've just lost my husband and both of my children, one by one, all since Richard dug up those damned tribal relics. What would you think?'

Harrison didn't think she really wanted to hear what he thought. He didn't reply.

'I want them returned as soon as possible so that they can be reburied under the stones.'

He made a mental note of her request. While he didn't

think it would make the slightest difference to the body count, he did know it could help her state of mind. She still had a grandson to think about.

'Did your daughter believe in the curse?'

She shook her head forcefully.

'Absolutely not. She was incredibly practical and down to earth. Thought it was all mumbo jumbo.'

'And yet she said she saw vampires,' Harrison interjected.

Margaret dropped her head and nodded.

'Even as a child, she'd never believed in things like that. She was the first to question Father Christmas, the Easter Bunny, and the Tooth Fairy. She just didn't buy into any of it. That doesn't make sense either.'

'She would understandably have been very upset by her father's death, but what was her state of mind like?'

'She adored her father. It had hit her hard. Like me, she just couldn't see how he'd have had a heart attack.'

'Had she spoken to anyone about it? Anyone in the village?'

'Not that I'm aware of, but she'd gone out into the village that day and so it's possible.'

'And your son?'

'He was beside himself. Losing his father was bad enough, but when Carole died...'

Harrison waited for Margaret to finish. It was essential in interviews like this that he allowed people time to think and speak. Experience had told him the most valuable information came this way.

'He was very upset, but he was also scared. He started saying that the curse would come for him next. I should have taken more notice, shouldn't I?'

Margaret looked up at Harrison. The pain of loss, guilt, and sheer defeat raked across her face.

He had to be careful what he said to console her. For someone so vulnerable, whose sense of reality had been totally skewed, there was no option to tell her that curses were indeed mumbo jumbo and what had killed her family was either a combination of natural co-incidences, or the work of somebody evil who had targeted them for reasons as yet unknown.

10

Back in the car, you could cut the atmosphere with a butter knife, although Harrison judged that DS Haynes might have preferred a large and very sharp sword.

'Well, what did she say?' He asked tersely, the second it became apparent that Harrison wasn't about to tell him anything.

'Factually, nothing different to what you have in the statements already...'

Haynes emitted a loud humph of "told you so".

'But,' continued Harrison, 'She was able to give me a good feel for the state of mind of each victim. I'd also like to speak to two people she mentioned, neither of whom appear to be on your list.'

Haynes's head snapped round from where he'd been sitting, jaw set, eyes forward, not even bearing to look at Harrison.

'The Vicar, and a Bob Williams,' Harrison continued.

'The Vicar? Why would you need to speak with Reverend Davenport?'

'He was party to a heated discussion that took place between Richard, Bob, and himself.'

'You're not suggesting that the Vicar...'

'In an enquiry, we keep an open mind. There are no suggestions, just the need to check everything.' Harrison was firm.

'I've been a police officer for thirty-four years, and a detective for fifteen. I know how investigations work,' DS Haynes spat back at him.

Harrison was tempted to retort with a question as to why he was still a DS then, but remained professional.

'Good. Then you will agree and we can go and see him now.'

There were a few moments of hesitation while it dawned on Haynes that he'd boxed himself into a corner, before he swallowed his pride and turned the key in the ignition. He said nothing more for the duration of the journey, but that suited Harrison just fine.

His driving was somewhat aggressive, but Harrison had experienced far worse. The rain, which had started earlier but increased in intensity, battered at the windscreen, necessitating the wiper blades to be on full speed for any clear visibility, for most of the journey. Their frenetic whining back and forth seemed to mirror the white knuckled mood of DS Haynes. By the time they'd reached their destination, the rain had at least eased, leaving a thin drizzle which coated their clothes in a shimmering sheen of tiny water droplets after they'd got out of the car.

They pulled up alongside the wall of the churchyard, where a large wooden sign proclaimed the times of the Christingle and Christmas Eve services, one in the afternoon for families, and the second at midnight for those older, more devoted attendees.

Haynes was certainly not displaying any Christmas spirit, and he got out of the car without a word. Harrison followed him down the road, past the gate to the church and to a wooden door which carried a sign saying, "Vicarage".

He went straight through and walked up a short garden path to a brown wooden front door, and knocked. Harrison stood behind him and they both waited. He could tell that Haynes was more than happy to turn around and leave when his knock went unanswered, but he was out of luck. As they were just about to go, the brown door swung open and a tall man in a black shirt and trousers with a white dog collar stood before them. Harrison estimated him to be in his late fifties, with a full head of sandy blonde hair that was greying at the temples. It wasn't a warm face. His features were stern and unforgiving, but he gave a thin smile to DS Haynes.

'Scott, how can I help you?'

'Brian, I'm here in an official capacity.'

The reverend raised his right eyebrow and peered at the large, muscular man behind him. The sight of Harrison clearly gave no clues.

'Yes?' He queried.

'This is Dr Harrison Lane,' DS Haynes finally acknowledged him, 'and he would like to ask you about a conversation you and Bob Williams had with Richard Templeton just before he died.'

'I'd also like to ask you about your vampire legend, too,' Harrison interjected.

The Reverend's face lit up at that request.

'No problem at all. Shall we go across to the church? I can show you the original ledgers that record the strange goings on in 1753.'

The Reverend Brian Davenport didn't wait for a

response. He stepped out of his door and pulled it closed behind him, after hooking a set of keys out of a china tray by the door. Harrison didn't feel it appropriate to tell him that this was not a sensible place to keep keys because any burglar worth his salt knew how to hook them up through the letterbox.

'How is Margaret doing?' Reverend Davenport asked.

'Struggling,' Haynes replied.

'Not surprising. I'll pop up tomorrow again and see how she is.'

'Did you know Richard Templeton well?' Harrison asked.

'Yes, he was a good supporter of the village, on our festival committee, and he let us use the house grounds for the autumn fair. Margaret came to church more often than Richard, but he was always happy to help when required. A fairly quiet man.'

'In your experience, was he a man who would have believed in curses, vampires, and superstitions?'

'No. I was surprised when I heard he'd been digging at the stones. We'd all assumed that was just a story about his grandfather burying treasure there.'

The three of them arrived at the entrance to the church, and Reverend Davenport unlocked the door with a large key.

'The origins of our church are 16th century, although there was a small monastery on this site before that. Additions were made to the church in the 1800s, thanks to the Templetons. You'll see that Richard's forebears have plaques along the wall inside, and theirs is the large white marble mausoleum in the graveyard. Every member of the family has been interred in there since it was built, although it's getting tight on space now, and I've suggested cremation where appropriate. Of course, we've not had Richard's funeral yet. Carole said her father hadn't shared any particular wishes with his family, but I think it was just presumed he'd be put in with the others.'

'You spoke to Carole?' Harrison picked up.

'Yes, she came to see me. Hadn't seen her in here since she was a little girl, but grief and tragedy are strong motivators for people to seek out the comfort of our Lord.'

'When was this?'

Reverend Davenport looked at him a moment longer than Harrison would have expected. It was difficult to see the thoughts going on behind his well-practiced, pious expression.

'Mmmh, let me think.' He pushed open the church door and stepped into the gloom.

Just inside the door was a small wooden nativity scene of the baby Jesus in the manger being visited by the Wise men. Harrison knew to resist the urge to say that the Wise Men didn't actually visit at the time of Jesus's birth, even Matthew in the Bible said that. However, he also knew that there was some poetic licence involved with Christmas imagery and facts weren't always the primary motivation.

'You can see the Templetons' plaques on the wall here on our right. We also have particularly fine examples of carved wooden pews. In most churches, they're quite plain.' The Reverend proudly prattled on as he led them down the aisle which had been decorated ready for the Christmas services.

'Was it straight after her father's death, or on the day she died? Her mother said she came into the village.' Harrison was more than keen to get the facts right about the current case and so he pushed, sensing the vicar was stalling and avoiding answering his question about Carole.

He appeared to think again for a few moments.

'Yes. I believe it was the day she was tragically taken from us.'

'Did she tell you she was going to the stones?'

'She mentioned she was going to take some flowers. Also asked me if I would go and see her mother. She was worried about her.'

'How did Carole seem in herself?'

'Upset, but under control. There was no hysteria.'

They were in the main body of the church now and Haynes had remained stony faced and silent throughout.

'The Reverend gave a very moving tribute to Richard and Carole on Sunday,' he said to Harrison, as though trying to head off any negative thoughts he might be having about the vicar. 'And it was very well received by everyone,' he added to the man himself, eager to compliment him.

'Thank you Scott. The curse has been good for business. Sorry, that sounded crass. I don't mean burials. I'm talking about the increase in our congregations. It's brought a lot more people through the doors.' He reddened and quickly turned away from Harrison.

'Shall we look at the files on the so-called vampire?' He walked swiftly off towards the back of the church and led them into a back room, before unlocking a large wooden cupboard. Inside were piles of ancient books and ledgers.

'Here it is. I had it out recently to show Bob Williams. He's been writing a history of the village and wanted to know as much detail about the alleged vampire as possible.'

Harrison was itching to ask him about the day of the argument, but instead let him talk. It was amazing what things someone might inadvertently say when there was silence to fill.

Reverend Davenport had opened the large leather-bound ledger he'd taken out of the cupboard and turned to a page that was already marked by a strip of paper.

'Here it is, September 1753, a Simon Mason had been due to be buried in the churchyard, but it was reported that the night before his burial, he arose from his coffin and terrorised the village, knocking on doors and moaning and groaning. The villagers hid in their houses and in the morning they gathered a party together, led by the curate, Thomas Smith, and they went in search of him. They found him back at his home, seemingly dead again but lying on his bed, not in his coffin, and there was blood trickling from his mouth. Outside in the street, they found a cat that had been savagely attacked and half eaten.'

'The vicar said a prayer and absolved the man of his sins, and he was hastily buried in the churchyard. That night, the villagers heard howling and again they were too scared to leave their homes. The following morning, a goat had been savagely attacked. This went on for several more nights until the villagers took matters into their own hands and dug up the coffin containing Simon Mason. The Curate had been against this action, but when they opened the coffin, they found blood oozing from the corpse's mouth and ears and his teeth had become like fangs, and his nails like claws. They impaled his heart with a spike and as they did so, he let out a groan and blood poured from the wound. So they cut off his head. There was some argument as to whether to burn his remains, but in the end, the ancient belief that the druid circle on the headland protected the village prevailed. They buried his remains beneath the largest stone so he could rise no more. The curate condemned their pagan beliefs, but was unable to explain what he had seen and reported it to his superiors. After Simon Mason was buried beneath the blood stone, the village was no longer terrorised by the vampire.'

Reverend Davenport closed the ledger and looked up at Harrison, raising his eyebrows.

'There are many stories like this around the world. Knowledge of medicine and what happens to the human body after death, were very primitive in those days.' Harrison said. 'Poor Simon Mason was probably not dead, but awoke from some kind of coma to find himself in his coffin. He obviously then tried to seek help but was probably delirious with dehydration and whatever had made him ill in the first place, and then did collapse and die. We also know that when a body decomposes, the gums will shrink back on the teeth, giving the impression that the teeth have grown, and this is the same with the nails. The blood oozing from his mouth and ears would have been the natural bodily fluids that the corpse expels as it decomposes, and the groan was the escaping of the gases as they pierced his body.' Harrison said to him, matter-of-factly.

'What about the animal deaths?' Haynes interjected. He'd been listening intently to the conversation.

'Likely a wolf or wild dog. Howling is mentioned, and there would have been wolves around the area in those times. The villagers simply did what humans are prone to do, they created a pattern of events and a story from a series of random occurrences.'

'Yes, I'd agree with Dr Lane on that. It was pagan mumbo jumbo. But, even to this day, the plot in which Simon Mason had been buried remains empty. No one wants to be buried there. Stories and the fear they incur, like this, live on.' Reverend Davenport added.

'When you referred to this all being good for business,

what did you mean, exactly?' Harrison turned to the reverend, who immediately resumed his bright red of earlier.

'That was a terrible turn of phrase. I merely meant that our congregation has been thinning of late and now we're getting a nearly full church each Sunday.'

'Why would that be?'

'Well, I think that in times of uncertainty and worry, people naturally turn to our Lord for comfort.'

'But this is one family who is mostly affected. Why are others in the village worried?'

'Around here, Dr Lane, there is a deep connection between the Templetons and the village. If they are in trouble, then people assume that trouble will impact the village. We have already seen another unexplained death, as you know.'

'Are you aware of any vampire cults, or people who celebrate the vampire legend locally?'

'No. No, not at all.' He shook his head vigorously.

Harrison changed tack.

'And what was it that caused the heated discussion between yourself, Bob, and Richard Templeton?'

Harrison watched the reverend's every mannerism, the slightly uncomfortable flutter of his hands seeking comfort and reassurance that what he was about to say was the right thing.

'Richard wasn't happy with Bob writing about his family. It was the first time they'd discussed it. I was keen because we are struggling as a church. Bob said it would bring attention to the village and so the church would benefit. I must admit that Bob should have been more thoughtful about what he was doing. He should have checked with

Richard first and got him onside. He'd have found it much easier that way.'

'Do you think Richard's motivation to dig at the stones could have been to dispel all the legends and scupper Bob's planned book?'

'I can't comment on that, I'm afraid. He never mentioned anything to me.'

'I'm going to need a statement from you.' DS Haynes stepped forward, his face set in a serious frown. 'How did Bob react to Richard's objections?'

Reverend Davenport looked even more uncomfortable now.

'I'm not intending to get Bob into trouble. It was just a conversation. They'd have worked out their differences, I'm sure.'

'Perhaps.' Harrison smiled at him and held his gaze for just a moment too long for Reverend Davenport, who once again looked embarrassed and uncomfortable, flushing red above his white dog collar.

'Thank you for your time,' Harrison added and walked back out through the church, leaving Reverend Davenport and Scott Haynes in his wake.

11

The welcome back at the station was a lot warmer than the atmosphere in the car on the drive there. Harrison wasn't pandering to DS Haynes's obvious bias with regard to the reverend. There was nothing worse than trying to investigate a case with someone who had preconceived ideas. He wasn't going to even attempt to paper over the cracks in their relationship either. It was clearly fractured and would remain so.

The DS, for his part, couldn't contain himself. 'I can't believe that you think the vicar might have something to do with it. You made him feel quite uncomfortable.'

Harrison sighed and contemplated ignoring him, but in the event, simply replied, 'We have to look at all possibilities.'

For the rest of the journey he looked out of the window, not wanting to engage in conversation. The last few weeks had been tough on him. The case in Jersey had been a harrowing one, and then there was the small matter of coming home to the revelations about his so-called father. It had knocked him for six. His primary concern, as always, was to focus and so he didn't want to let emotion get in the way of his thought processing. DS Haynes was winding him up. That showed Harrison he wasn't as focused as he should be. He thought about the quiet privacy of his apartment in London. He needed to meditate, to centre himself and rebuild his resilience. Tonight he would try to do that, for now he just had to ignore Haynes and try not to get irritated by him. Harrison focused on his breathing, calming his mind.

When they got back into the incident room, all the rest of the team were there and DI Christie looked up expectantly. Harrison saw him register the look on Haynes's face and also noted there wasn't surprise, he was clearly used to dealing with him. 'Shall we have a quick team update?' Christie hopefully suggested.

Harrison nodded and followed him into the room they'd met in earlier.

They had a few moments before the rest of the team caught up with them.

'Is everything alright? DS Haynes assisting you?' Adam Christie asked Harrison quietly.

'It's fine,' he'd replied.

His answer seemed to appease the detective's fears, but either way, the arrival of the rest of the team put paid to any further discussion.

'Now that you've had a chance to review the situation, I wondered if you might have some initial thoughts to share with the team? I'd also like to share with you some of the potential suspects and motives we've been looking at. *If* this is actually a murder investigation.' DI Christie said.

'Dr Lane seems to think the Vicar might be involved,' Haynes couldn't contain himself, and nobody in the room would have missed the mix of venom and sarcasm in his voice.

'I'm looking at all the potential possibilities' said Harrison.

Haynes humphed, 'what potential motive could the vicar have to harm Richard Templeton?'

'His church congregation has been dwindling. I saw an announcement on the notice board at the front of the church that the diocese are thinking about closing the church down. Now all of a sudden he tells me that the church is full, people are scared about the vampire and curse rumours. Indeed, his own words were, that it's been good for business. An increase in his congregation would make it much easier for Reverend Davenport to keep the church open, and for him to keep his job. We have to look at everyone who could gain from this situation. If Richard was attempting to disprove the legends of curses and vampires, then he might have been a threat.'

Haynes didn't need to say anything, his face said it all. A look of intense disgust and shock clawed across his features. Harrison thought he might explode and was ashamed to realise that he would enjoy the spectacle. DI Christie stepped in.

'I think at this stage of the enquiry we have to look at every possibility, as Dr Lane said. Nobody is suggesting that the vicar is a murderer, but we have to look at every potential motive for what's happened to Richard Templeton and the rest of his family.'

'Then the clearest suspect is still John Rowland, he wanted to buy that house and Richard said no, he's been asking him for years.'

'John has just lost Lee too,' retorted Christie. 'Do you think he killed his own son as well?'

Haynes pursed his lips and let out a frustrated sigh like an adolescent.

'So, Dr Lane any thoughts after speaking to Margaret Templeton?' Christie continued, clearly used to Scott Haynes's temperament.

'I'm still not sure if it's a series of unconnected occurrences, or the work of one or more individuals. There are potential motives. We need to speak to Bob Williams about an argument he and Richard had just before he died. The vicar was also part of that.'

To his right, DS Haynes crossed his arms over his chest and purposely looked out of the window.

Harrison continued regardless. 'Margaret said Richard was a man who avoided conflict. He'd clearly got upset about the fact that Bob Williams was writing a book about his family. While we know there's no history or any indications of problems with his heart, people who avoid conflict often suffer greater anxiety and stress because they internalise their worries. It's possible that the family concerns over money and the latest issue with the book tipped Richard over the edge and he simply had a heart attack. However, I don't understand why he chose now to go and dig up what his grandfather buried underneath the stones. Margaret said they'd had money issues all their lives, and also that the children had offered to help them out with the roof costs, so the money motive doesn't make sense. Have the arrow and spear heads been analysed by the lab?' Harrison looked to the team.

'Yes, we're not amateurs. They've been checked out, nothing more than some old tribal souvenirs.' Haynes interrupted. 'They're not precious metals or anything like that.'

'Was that all he found?' Harrison asked, 'Could there be

a possibility that he found something else and that somebody could have taken it? Perhaps something that was valuable and worth killing for?'

'We've no evidence of that at all. When we looked at the ground where he'd been digging there certainly wasn't any indication that anything else had been in the hole. It looks like he literally just found the spear and arrow heads, unwrapped them to look at them, and died.' Replied Christie.

'Unwrapped them?'

'Yes, they were wrapped in some kind of leather cloth.'

Harrison nodded thoughtfully. He'd need to look at the heads and the forensic report on them before he could make any judgement.

'What about Carole?' Christie pressed.

'She visited the village, including speaking to Reverend Davenport,' he added just to spike Haynes, 'prior to going up to the stones. Nobody, so far, thinks that she believed in the curse or vampires, so I still don't have any explanation for the phone recording. I'd like to run some more tissue tests just to check for other, perhaps more unusual, hallucinants.'

DI Christie nodded. 'Whatever you need. We need to track down everybody she saw before she went up to those stones. If it's someone in the village who is doing this, then it's possible they administered something before she went up there. John, order some extensive tests, will you? Tell them we're looking for any kind of hallucinant or poison, natural or chemical.' Christie said.

'Sure thing.' Sergeant Cutter nodded.

'I also think we should have some kind of protection for Margaret. Get a family liaison up there to log everyone coming and going and to keep an eye on things. If there's a police presence, then any perpetrator might think twice before attempting to harm her.'

'Good idea. I know Reverend Davenport is due to go and see her, and while we are not saying he is definitely a suspect, I'm sure he won't be the only person visiting to pay their respects, or perhaps finish what they started.' Harrison replied.

'I looked into whether there'd been any other sudden deaths in the area,' DC Lucy Robinson spoke up now. 'There was one other death, just over a week ago, which would fit in with our timeline.'

'Thanks Lucy, we'd better check that out too, if this isn't a series of coincidences then there might be others who have been impacted by whatever is going on.' DI Christie said to the team, and Harrison, who didn't disagree.

12

Ryan prided himself on finding anything there was to find on the internet. If it was there, even if it had been deleted, he could usually find it. Hunting vampires wasn't something Harrison had asked him to do before, but he was damned sure it wasn't going to beat him. He was, however, finding it tough, and the spent carcasses of snack packets were threatening to turn into an avalanche on his desk.

He expected to find the Goth fetish groups. He still remembered his own school friends' fascination and obsession with the Twilight series of books and the vampires they talked about as though they were the sexiest creatures ever. He made contact with a few groups in the area, but there were none which fitted the description given by Carole Templeton, or who were likely to have been near to the stones that night.

He also made contact with every drama group he could find, including students, but every one led to a dead end.

What Ryan hadn't realised was that there is more than one type of person who revels in the vampire culture. He managed to find several groups of people who declared themselves as needing to drink blood. While it wasn't as prevalent in the UK as it was in the United States, where thousands of people claimed to regularly drink human blood, he had discovered a hidden network of self-help and support groups of those who were not believers in the supernatural, and many weren't even doing it for some kind of fetish ritual, but believed themselves to have a medical condition which required regular blood drinking.

As Ryan read their conversations in the secret channels, it was clear they included people who held responsible jobs in society. There were nurses, accountants, secretaries, and bus drivers. They hid because of the fear that others wouldn't understand their needs and instead see them as a danger, and he could understand why. The thought he might live next door to someone like that gave him the creeps. They might use consenting donors and follow strict hygiene rules, but it was still something which he found abhorrent. Feeding off human blood was just plain weird and disgusting in his mind.

Having said that, suffering from his own seemingly irrational fear of open spaces as he did, Ryan never dismissed another person's medical issues, physical or mental, and he could understand why they'd want to keep this particular issue under wraps and why others would want to avoid them. It wouldn't be an easy topic around the work water cooler. "what did you do last night? Oh, just invited a friend round so I could drink a few shots of their blood."

The groups were highly secretive and so it wasn't easy to infiltrate, but eventually, he was satisfied that none of the people in the area were likely to have been at the stones that evening. For one thing, they didn't dress up in the mock vampire clothing that Carole had described. He was running out of options. Who would dress up as vampires and meet somewhere like that? If it wasn't a drama group, a goth vampire fetish meet up, or a real human blood drinker, then who could it be and did they even exist, or had Carole imagined it?

One person who Ryan knew hadn't been imagined was Desmond Manning, who'd crawled under a rock somewhere after making his boss's life a misery and killing a man to frame him. It was about seven in the evening, and Ryan was just thinking about heading home and starting his vampire hunt afresh in the morning, when an email arrived that gave him his best clue yet as to exactly which rock it was that Desmond was hiding under. He was close on his heels now. Tantalisingly close.

13

The bungalow was in a neat road that curved around into a horseshoe shape. All the properties were single storey, built in the days when developers were generous with garden space. Harrison could imagine that in the summer, the whole road would be alight with colour. Mature bushes and trees lined the paths, and the gardens were mostly well kept and well stocked, the telltale hallmark of people retired and able to enjoy their leisure time and properties.

'It's number fourteen,' DS Scott Haynes said, and craned to look at the house numbers, slowing the car. Harrison had been reluctant to have to head back out with the DS, but Adam Christie asked if he would go with him to check out the additional sudden death case which DC Lucy Robinson had found.

Harrison pointed a little further along on the right side. It was one of the neatest houses and gardens. A white painted bungalow with what looked to be climbing roses in the summer, a neatly manicured lawn, and tidy flower beds. Even in winter there was colour; winter jasmine gave a splash of yellow amid the evergreen and browns. The path was finished with edging stones like twisted rope, and there were two neat blue pots on either side of the entrance door, which was a white plastic double glazed porch. Through its side windows, Harrison could see a row of ceramic plates hanging on the wall.

The owners of this property liked order. As Harrison and DS Haynes walked up the path, he could see the bushes were pruned and trimmed to perfection. Their love of order stretched to trying to control nature, and even before they knocked on the front door, he could already guess at the kind of interior furnishings they were about to be invited into.

A slender woman with a silver grey bob haircut and wearing what looked like new jeans and a bright red poppy jumper opened the door and smiled at them. There was nervousness in her face. Harrison could see that immediately. The smile was warm and genuine, but its edges were ragged with anxiety.

'Mrs Paulson?' Haynes held out his police ID. 'DS Scott Haynes and Dr Harrison Lane. Our colleague, DC Robinson called earlier.'

'Yes. Come in.'

Harrison could almost hear Haynes's approval as they were shown into Mrs Paulson's sitting room. Parker Knoll recliners were separated by a traditional English sofa with deep seats and a high sprung back, rolled arms and covered in a duck egg blue fabric. Haynes bee-lined the sofa, settling into it like a hen returning to her nest. In front of him was a bookcase with the Bible prominently displayed - both new and old testaments - and what looked like a silver plaque of the Last Supper mounted on wood.

Harrison sat down next to him, avoiding the two chairs

which presumably were the favoured seating for Mrs Paulson and her recently deceased husband.

'Can I get you both a tea?' She timidly asked, looking from one to the other.

'I would love a cup, thank you,' DS Haynes replied, settling back further into the sofa and smiling broadly at their host.

'Milk and sugar?'

'A touch of each.'

Mrs Paulson looked at Harrison expectantly.

'A glass of water will be fine, thank you.'

She didn't waste any time, but bustled out of the room.

'Nice woman,' the DS pronounced with satisfaction. 'Don't see how this could be connected to our case, but we'd better follow orders.'

Harrison said nothing. He looked out the sitting-room window to the back garden, where the offending hedge stood shamelessly. It was half trimmed, although in all honesty, the section that hadn't received a haircut wasn't starkly different to that which had.

'Here you are. I do hope it's how you wanted it.' Their host returned, handing Harrison his glass of water and placing a teacup and saucer on the table next to Haynes. Harrison noticed she didn't put it on the coaster which sat by the side of the saucer. When she went back out of the room to fetch her own tea, Haynes absentmindedly slid the coaster over and under his tea to protect the table.

'Firstly, Mrs Paulson, our condolences for your loss.' He began as she returned. 'We don't want to take up too much of your day at this difficult time.'

Mrs Paulson sat softly onto one of the recliners and looked at them both intently, perched on the edge, back straight.

'Thank you,' she almost whispered. 'Is your tea alright?'

DS Haynes nodded.

'Yes, thanks. As I explained on the phone, we're investigating a series of unexplained deaths, and as part of that investigation, we've been asked to look into any other accidental or unusual deaths in the past few weeks. I don't want to cause you any distress, but would you kindly talk us through the events that led up to your husband's accident?'

'I did tell the other police officers at the time, is there something wrong?'

'I know, and as I said, I apologise for having to ask you again. There's nothing wrong. It's just we need to rule out your husband's accident from our enquiries.'

Mrs Paulson looked nervously at Harrison, who hadn't said a word since she'd re-entered the room. He smiled reassuringly at her.

'Douglas was cutting the hedge. He was a stickler for making sure it didn't grow out of shape, couldn't bear disorder or things not being kept tidy. He was a very...' she paused, trying to find the right word, 'very particular man. He had me helping him and as usual, I'd been assigned the clear-up duties. I was picking up some twigs and putting them into garden waste sacks when I heard a bang and turned to see he'd been knocked off the ladder. He'd cut through the electricity cable. Doctor said it gave him a heart attack. Killed him instantly.'

'Hmm, does your husband have any connection to the Templetons?'

She looked quizzical and shook her head.

'Absolutely sure there isn't a family connection, or he never worked for them?'

'I'm sure.'

'Do you have any idea how he could have made such an error with the lead?'

Mrs Paulson looked down at her hands in her lap, and her fingers which were twisting around each other.

'He'd told me to pick up the pieces a few feet away, didn't want me getting underneath where he was trimming. Said he didn't want to waste time in A and E if I got hurt because the rugby was due on in an hour. Usually he gets me to keep an eye out.'

'So perhaps he was rushing and wasn't as careful as usual?'

'Perhaps,' she mumbled. Her eyes shot quickly to Harrison and then back to DS Haynes.

'And you didn't use a circuit breaker?' He pressed.

'Not that day. Like you said, it was because he was in a bit of a hurry,' she replied, rubbing her palms on her thighs. She didn't lift her eyes at all, but kept them focused on her hands.

Harrison had been looking around the room and noticed a distinct absence of photographs, and apart from the bookcase, very few ornaments and pictures.

'Do you have a photograph of your husband, Mrs Paulson?' he asked.

She looked almost shocked that he'd spoken and jumped up from her chair as though the shockwave had shot up from the seat and gone right through her.

'Yes,' she replied and crossed over to a sideboard, pulling open the top drawer and taking out a silver photo frame. She handed it to Harrison and went to sit down again.

He looked at the image in front of him. They appeared to be at a wedding. The pair of them dressed smartly. He was in a suit, the shirt not only ironed, but Harrison would guess it had also been starched. She wore a small, understated hat and a flowery dress with a plain peach jacket. Behind them, he could just make out a crowd of other similarly dressed people, in what looked like a large garden area.

'Wedding?' Harrison asked, smiling encouragingly.

'Yes, Douglas's nephew,' then she looked a little panicked. 'Our nephew, his brother's son.'

He looked back down at the photo. Douglas was beaming at the camera. He looked not much over five feet six, at most, just an inch or so taller than his wife. He had hold of her hand, but it wasn't a relaxed pose. He held on to her tightly, pulling her arm down straight as though bringing her to his side by force. Mrs Paulson's face was smiling for the camera, but it was the kind of smile that looked fixed and didn't come from within. Harrison passed it to DS Haynes.

'Lovely photograph,' the DS said, looking at it briefly and passing it back to Mrs Paulson. 'We have to hold on to those happy memories in times like these,' he added with forced sincerity.

Harrison wondered how the man could be so unobservant.

'How long were you married, Mrs Paulson?' Harrison asked.

'Thirty-three years. I was his second marriage.'

'No children?'

'No. He'd had a son with his first wife and didn't see the need for anymore.' Her eyes held his gaze for a moment before dropping back to her lap. 'It doesn't matter now.'

'No, absolutely,' Haynes interrupted, giving Harrison a hard stare. 'We're here to ascertain the cause of your husband's tragic accident, not stir up the past.'

'Would you mind if I used your toilet?' Harrison asked.

She hesitated a moment and then seemed to swallow her objection.

'Of course, it's the second door on the right.'

He got up to leave just as Haynes launched into a conversation about which church they attended.

Harrison looked into the kitchen from the hallway; there were a few plates and cups on the side by the sink. Not unusual necessarily for someone bereaved and not functioning as normal, but he didn't feel that Mrs Paulson would have left them there like that unless she'd wanted to.

As he turned down the short corridor to the bedrooms, he was met by the sight of several black bin liners, filled. Harrison peered inside and saw they were full of men's clothing, along with some women's dresses. At the pretence of not remembering which door she'd told him to go to, he pushed open the first door on the left. It was the main bedroom. A pink floral duvet cover was on the bed. It looked new, with the creased look of something just taken out of the packet. There were some shopping bags on the floor too that were filled with brand new women's trousers and tops. In the room, ornaments and pictures had also been taken from sight, and he could see some of them stacked in boxes. The wardrobe had been almost decimated. Most of the hangers were empty.

Harrison quickly went into the toilet and flushed it, making as if he was washing his hands after, before returning to the sitting room. Haynes was still talking church matters with Mrs Paulson, who looked nervously at Harrison as he re-entered.

'If you don't mind, could I also use your facilities?' Haynes asked. 'Bladder isn't quite what it used to be.'

'Of course,' she'd replied and then took to studying her hands on her lap as he left the room.

'Was it you who plugged in the hedge cutter?' Harrison asked.

She gave an almost imperceptible nod.

'You're having a clear out,' he broached, stating the fact.

Tears brimmed in her eyes.

'There's a charity coming round tomorrow to pick up all his things.'

'And your dresses?'

'I never liked wearing them,' she said to him, an edge of defiance in her eyes now and she jutted out her chin. 'He didn't want me wearing trousers. It had to be dresses and skirts.'

Harrison raised an eyebrow to encourage her to say more.

'It was never physical, you know. In public, everyone thought he was the perfect husband. Very attentive, but that was so he could keep an eye on me.'

'Did you ever try to leave?'

'I thought about it every day, but how could I? He controlled all our money. He didn't like me socialising. I had no friends to go to, and I was an only child.'

Harrison nodded at her in sympathy. The evidence of her husband's controlling nature was all around him, in the house, the garden, the photograph she'd shown him, and her recent attempt to eradicate that control from her life following his death.

'Are you going to arrest me?' She asked him with a big sigh.

The pair of them heard the door to the toilet unlock and knew that DS Haynes would rejoin them at any moment. Harrison had a split second decision to make. Tell him his suspicions; he knew that Mrs Paulson would confess instantly. She'd spent years of being conditioned to be compliant. But who would that serve? She was no danger to anyone else. Did she deserve to spend the last years of her life locked in a cell, after spending most of it trapped in a controlling marriage? Apart from her confession, there would be no evidence to say what had actually happened. Just her saying that she'd not plugged in the circuit breaker and had probably failed to warn her husband that the lead was in the way. No judge or jury was likely to convict on that evidence, anyway. At the end of the day, her husband cut the lead himself. It was an accident.

'We'd better get going,' Haynes said, walking in on the pair of them and looking from one to the other. 'Everything alright?'

'Yes, absolutely fine,' Harrison replied, smiling at Mrs Paulson. 'I'm sorry we took up your time. You must have a lot to sort out. I think we can rule out your husband's death from our enquiries. There's no connection. I hope you are able to find a way through this difficult time and that you'll eventually be able to enjoy your life again.'

The tears brimmed over her eyes as she looked at him in gratitude.

Harrison wondered when the last time was that anyone had shown her kindness.

'Yes, absolutely. Don't you worry, we'll see ourselves out and won't be bothering you again. Sorry to have disturbed you at this difficult time.' Haynes added with a tone that was potentially well meaning, but served to sound condescending instead.

They left her blowing her nose into a tissue.

'Poor love, she must be devastated,' DS Haynes said as they headed back to the car.

'At least we can rule this one out from our investigation,' Harrison replied, giving one last look to the bungalow. He expected that by this time next year, it would look quite different, inside and out.

'Agreed. Knew this would be a wild goose chase. I hope she'll be able to manage that place now her husband has gone.' Haynes added.

Harrison marvelled again at how unobservant the man could be.

14

The next visit on their list was John Rowland. Harrison was well aware of what Scott Haynes thought about him. DI Christie had warned Scott prior to them going out that he had to remember John was grieving, so Harrison hoped he would keep himself under control.

John Rowland was the village GP, and his home was next door to the surgery, which was situated in the centre of the village. It was the largest house in the village, well kept and English chocolate box pretty, even in the winter. A large Christmas wreath was on the front door, but Harrison guessed their festivities this year would now be severely tempered.

John wasn't working, having only lost his son three days ago, so they pulled into the GP car park and walked across to the house. The door was answered by a woman in her fifties, thin and fit and clearly an active sports woman. Today she looked drawn and pale, her eyes puffy and pink, and she'd made no effort to look presentable. Her clothes were merely on for decency's sake.

'Eileen, so sorry for your loss,' DS Haynes said, giving Harrison some hope that he would behave himself. 'I spoke to John earlier, said we'd be round as we're looking into all unexplained deaths in the area.'

'Come in, John's in his study. Go on through to the sitting room and I'll get him.'

Eileen Rowland was on autopilot, going through the motions of being a good host. In her, Harrison could see the true ravages of grief which had ripped out her heart and stamped on it. She was a mother who'd lost a son. The natural order of life and death disrupted and upended.

Their sitting room was comfortable and lived-in. There was no evidence of an over-controlling personality here. Harrison could see family photographs mixed in with holiday souvenirs, and tasteful antique ornaments and furniture. This was clearly a family home and there was love in abundant evidence, from the slogans on the cushions, to the candid shots of Eileen and John, or the pair of them with younger versions of themselves. He assumed the young lad in the images was the unfortunate Lee.

DS Haynes saw Harrison looking at the photographs.

'They've got a daughter as well. She was at Uni when it happened.'

From the corridor, they heard hushed voices approaching and a tall man with a neat beard led Eileen back into the room. Harrison and DS Haynes put their hands out in greeting. The bearded man grasped Harrison's first.

'John Rowland.'

'Dr Harrison Lane,' he replied, not missing the distasteful look John threw at Haynes.

'Scott,' John nodded and briefly shook his hand, before he and his wife moved to the sofa and sat down together.

Their body language was clear, huddled in to each other and holding hands. They were a team supporting each other. Both of them looked to Harrison and avoided Haynes, so Harrison took the lead. He guessed that Scott had already been round the house since their son's death, and the meeting hadn't gone well.

'I'm sorry for your loss and for disturbing you at this time, but I'm sure you're aware that we're looking into a number of unexplained deaths in the area, and I'd like to ask you a few questions surrounding the circumstances of your son's tragic death.'

They both nodded.

'I'm aware that you're a doctor, so did you ever have any reason to suspect that Lee was experiencing any kind of cardiac arrhythmia prior to his death?'

'None whatsoever. If I had, then we would have insisted he get it checked out immediately. He never once complained of any issues. I know the signs: dizziness, lightheadedness, shortness of breath, chest pain, etc. We saw nothing that would have worried us and he didn't tell us about any problems.' John replied.

'He played rugby,' Eileen interjected, 'he was fit and healthy. They were doing really well as a team and he was hoping they were going to go up a division this season.'

'And Lee still lived at home with you?'

'Some of the time, yes. He stayed over quite often at his girlfriend's house, Lizzie Meyer. She and her mother run the hairdressers in the village.'

'Did Lee have anything to do with the Templetons?'

'What do you mean?' John became defensive, sitting upright and taking his hand away from his wife's and instead grasping both his knees.

'As you know, three members of the Templeton family

have recently died and we are trying to see if there is any connection between their deaths and that of your son, or any others in the area.'

'You mean the damned curse that everyone is so scared of?' John curled his lip in disgust at the mention of it. 'The only curse on that family is the greed of Henry Templeton and the short-sightedness of Richard. Henry thought nothing about anyone other than himself. I'm sure you know how two men from the village were killed in one of his hair brained schemes?'

'Yes.' Harrison merely replied.

'Well, one of them was my grandfather.'

Harrison waited to see if there was any more that John wanted to get off his chest.

'I'd nothing against Richard, don't get me wrong, he was doing his best, but his father had spent the family fortune by the time he inherited and they're struggling with that place now. I offered to buy it, but he always refused.'

'Yes, I wanted to ask you about that. I understand there was an argument about purchasing the estate the day before Richard died.'

'It wasn't an argument, just the usual pig headedness from Richard. He refused to see that he was drowning in debt and I could offer a way out that would keep the estate for the village. There's a hotel company baying at his door, you know. They want the place. Had offered him a reasonable sum too, but I offered more. He refused to sell to anyone. Now poor Margaret is without any of them and she's going to have to deal with the mess on her own. We could easily lose the estate to some hotel conglomerate.'

Eileen Rowland reached out for her husband's hand, which was now balled in a fist on his knee. Her touch broke him from his rant, and he glanced at her with a weak smile before taking her hand and sitting back into the sofa.

'Carole Templeton came into the village on the day she died, did you meet with her at all?'

'Carole? No. Hadn't seen her in a while. She'd disappeared up to London and was working hard, by all accounts.'

'And were any of the Templetons patients of yours?'

John shook his head.

'No. They were with the surgery over at Roeburton. Dr Andrew Gillespie.'

'And how was Lee the night before he died? Was he behaving normally?'

'He was tired, went to bed early. Said he hadn't been sleeping well,' Eileen spoke up. She glanced at her husband. 'I think he was worried about the talk of the curse. He told me that it was all they were talking about at Lizzie's salon. He'd been with Lizzie for a few nights and come home in the hope he might get a better sleep. I think she was getting quite het up about it too.'

John was shaking his head.

'Bloody nonsense. Have we really not advanced since the 1800s? Shows you the level of average intelligence these days if all people can do is watch those awful reality dating shows and get worked up about some ancient curse.'

Harrison had to agree with John Rowland's sentiments, although he wondered if he'd missed the fact that by definition this could include his late son.

'So Lee went to bed early, and you heard nothing more from him?'

Eileen gave her head a minute shake and tears welled up in her eyes. John took up the story.

'I found him the next morning. Went in to see why he

wasn't up for work. He must have died in his sleep because he'd been gone a couple of hours by then.' John's voice wavered and cracked as he finished speaking. Harrison could see he was trying to persuade himself it was someone else, a patient, and he had to be detached and professional, but it wasn't. It was his twenty-five year old son, and that was too hard a fact to avoid.

Harrison paused a moment to allow the broken parents before him to recover.

'I have another question, a professional one,' he started, 'are you aware of any patients who suffer from haematomania or identify as vampires in any way? I appreciate patient confidentiality, but we are looking for a local group, or someone who believes it necessary to drink human blood. Or perhaps anyone who has a psychological disorder and believes in them or thinks themselves one?'

'Vampires!?' John exclaimed, looking at Harrison astonished. 'Absolutely not. No. Drinking blood can lead to all sorts of medical issues like hemochromatosis, an overload of iron, or even problems with the liver and other organs. Most people can't physically drink it anyway. We aren't built to drink blood, and it makes us retch.'

'Yes. I appreciate that, but there are some people who believe they have a medical need to do so.'

'Well, I can assure you that none of my patients are that way inclined.' John replied. 'All this rubbish about a vampire being buried under the blood stone. It's just that, rubbish.'

Harrison appreciated Dr Rowland's scientific take on the situation, although he wondered how much he took into account the psychological ailments of an individual, and not just their physical ones. They were equally important. However, he wasn't about to get into a debate about it right now, as the man was grieving and emotional. Rationality often went out the window for the bereaved, even if they were a doctor by profession.

He gave his thanks and left the Rowlands in peace, feeling a weight lift from him as he stepped back outside into the crisp December air.

'We could have another Harold Shipman on our hands with that one,' Haynes muttered as they returned to the car.

Harrison shivered, but he wasn't sure if it was the cold air or the icy chill of death hanging over them, which made his spine tingle.

15

Harrison was relieved to escape DS Haynes and his selfish piety. By the time they'd driven back to the incident room, the rain had started again with a vengeance, and it was dark. The small rural police station, which was housing their incident room, was mostly in darkness itself. Reception was shut and the car park virtually empty. Coverage for emergencies would be coming from the city cops. Harrison had no idea where he was staying that evening and so he'd headed back in to find DI Christie, who he hoped would provide him with an answer. Scott Haynes muttered about needing to get home and disappeared out the door with what Harrison presumed to be his packed lunch box.

DC Lucy Robinson and Sergeant John Cutter were just wrapping up for the night.

'Can I help you with anything, Dr Lane?' Lucy asked Harrison.

'No, I'm fine thank you.' Harrison replied.

He thought she seemed a little disappointed at his reply, but carried on towards Christie's desk.

Behind him, Lucy noted that Dr Harrison Lane had changed out of his black bike leathers, and was in a brushed cotton shirt with tan coloured chinos. His ample thighs filled the trouser legs and she couldn't help stealing a look at his tight rounded buttocks which were topped with broad muscular shoulders. She'd bet a week's worth of lunches that his six-pack was to die for. She reproached herself for the fact he was a good ten or more years older than herself, and that she was engaged to be married, but what was the harm? She was only looking.

Once her eyes had got their ample fill, she reengaged her brain and picked up her bag and coat.

'Night,' she called out to everyone and left them to it.

'How were John and Eileen?' Christie asked as Harrison reached him.

'As you'd expect. Devastated.'

'Anything useful out of it?'

'Everything is useful. I just need to piece it all together to see the full picture. Mr Paulson's death is unrelated. We can cross that off the list.'

Adam Christie sighed and leaned back in his chair.

'Maybe this is just one big wild goose chase.'

'No. Something is going on. I don't know what yet, but we could save other lives if we can get to the bottom of it. Your instincts are right.'

Adam nodded. He looked tired.

'Thanks, I'm battling internal pressures here. You know what it's like with budgets. I really appreciate your help on this. Fresh eyes and especially expert ones like yours are what we need. You've got a room booked at the pub in the village. It's quite nice there, they did a refurb of the rooms last year so all ensuite and mod cons. The food's good too. Sally does a mean lasagne.'

'I look forward to it,' Harrison replied.

'OK. Just turn right out of the station and head past the little supermarket and the hairdressers. You'll see it on the left-hand side, The Druid's Arms.'

HARRISON HAD MIXED feelings about being in a pub. Ordinarily it wouldn't bother him, his resolve and control were strong, but right now he didn't fully trust himself. He never drank. That was a given for anyone who knew him, but only his stepfather, Joe, knew the real reason why. After his mother's death, he'd gone completely feral, dropping out of society and living wild in the Welsh hills. The police had tried to look for him, but they never stood a chance and gave up. Even in the state that he was in, the skills his Shadow Wolf step father had taught him kept him hidden. Of course, after Joe had flown all the way from Arizona to find him, he had no hope. He tracked him down instantly, the same way he tracked the drug runners that tried to cross the Mexican/US border, using the Native American hunting skills that his own father had passed on to him.

Harrison could still remember that day. He'd stolen a bottle of vodka from a farmhouse, along with a small amount of food, and he was lying comatose in a damp cave in the Welsh hills. He was close to hypothermia, but he hadn't cared and the alcohol meant he wasn't aware, even if he had. When Joe had walked into that cave entrance, filling the doorway and blocking the light, he'd thought he was dreaming, or maybe that he was even dead already. It was only when Joe had embraced him, and he'd felt his warm skin against his, the roughness of his stubble and the damp of his tears, that's when he'd realised he was real.

Then it had all come out. The pain, the fears, the

loneliness, had poured out of him in a howl. The sound of an injured wolf when he'd been a child back home with Joe. They'd sat wrapped in each other's arms, Joe rocking him back and forth as the howling poured from him. Minute after agonising minute. Until finally the vodka and the emotion settled into his head, banging at his skull and he was exhausted.

Joe had helped him out of the cave and taken him to a small cottage he was renting. There, he never once judged him or criticised him, he never lectured him or told him what he should or shouldn't have done. Instead, he sat with him, meditating, healing his soul, centring his psyche, and helping him to find himself and his purpose in life. They'd followed the ancient ways of the Tohono O'odham tribe, connecting with nature, understanding it, not trying to control it. A tradition born out of learning to survive in the harsh desert conditions of their homeland.

Harrison hadn't touched a drop of alcohol since and his core had stayed strong, impenetrable. Until now. Now the doubts were creeping in. Had he really known his mother? What was her relationship with the man who was his genetic father? How could she have loved a man like that?

He was starting to drift from his rock. Tonight he could resist the temptation of losing his pain in a bottle, but he needed to speak to Joe, to feel his hand reach out across the Atlantic and pull him back to shore. The only man who had ever been a father to him. He needed him now.

Under normal circumstances, Harrison might have looked forward to listening to the general gossip in the Druids Arms bar in the hope it might shed some light on what was going on in the village. When he pushed open the door to the pub, he found it already more than half filled with a variety of people. Groups of youngsters huddled in gaggles, and old timers sat in the corner chewing the cud. It was a true village pub, probably the only place for miles where you didn't need to worry about drinking and driving because you could walk home. It was obvious the place had undergone a bit of a facelift, but they kept as much of a traditional bar as feasibly possible. So many pubs were struggling these days, but this one was clearly not one of them. There was a section through an arch which looked like it was the dining area. Tables were set out with some people already sitting and eating. Behind the bar was a young lad, blond, in his early twenties, and an older, darker-haired woman. Harrison presumed she might be the famed lasagna maker, Sally.

'Hi Sally? I have a room booked.'

'Sallys out back in the kitchen, I'll go get her for you,' the woman said.

'I'll get her.' The lad added helpfully and quickly turned to leave.

He returned almost immediately with a blond woman who had more than a passing resemblance to him, and Harrison surmised it must be mother and son. It was only when he saw the slight gesture of affection that Sally gave to the other woman that he realised they were probably the co-landlords.

'Dr Lane?' Sally said beaming widely. 'Welcome to the Druids Arms. I'm Sally Henshaw and this is Matt my son and my partner Penny. We hope you have a comfortable stay here. I understand you're booked with us for two nights initially with the possibility of an extension?'

'That's correct,' Harrison replied.

'We've got you in the Stone Circle room, that's a double

with ensuite shower and I have you down as joining us for dinner this evening?'

'Thank you, that would be fine.'

'What time would you like to eat?'

'I might go for a run first, so 8pm?'

'In this weather? That's dedication,' she said to him, eyebrows raised. '8pm it is. Your room is upstairs, and it's the first on the right.' Sally smiled again, handing him a set of keys with a piece of granite on the keyring.

Harrison headed through the doorway she'd pointed to, leaving the noise of the bar behind him. Up the staircase and to a corridor where he found a door with "Stone Circle" written on a wooden plaque. The room was exactly as DI Christie had said it would be, spotless and freshly redecorated with a brand-new bathroom. Harrison ignored the TV, as usual, and went across to the window, pulling the curtains against the rain, which was yet again hammering hard on the glass as it thrashed down to earth from the heavens.

It had been a long day: travelling, trying to get his head around the case, and the emotional aftermath of the previous 24 hours. He dropped his bag on the floor, sat down on the bed, and texted Joe. They were seven hours ahead in Arizona, so Joe was probably at work. He might not be free to talk.

Harrison was too agitated to settle and meditate, so he decided to go for a run. Running helped him feel free, to give his mind a break and his body the chance to expend any tension that had built up. He craved the pain of the exertion, the rhythmic pounding of his feet and the thumping of his heart that reminded him to live in the here and now and not in the past.

He stripped down to his underwear and dug around in

his bag for the running shorts and t-shirt he'd put in that morning. Then he hooked out his trainers and put them on, before doing a few stretches. The air would be cold on his muscles, he needed them to be warmed up before he asked too much of them.

When he went down the stairs, he saw a door at the bottom, which meant he didn't need to go through the bar to get out. It had a lock on it which explained the second key on the keyring Sally had given him. Harrison opened the door and felt the blast of icy air and rain fly straight into his face and on his exposed arms and legs. He didn't hesitate. He pulled it shut behind him and stepped out into the night and the main street which ran through the village.

It was darker here than running through the London streets. Although there were streetlights, there was less light pollution from the big sprawling city, and so the sky, which was already covered in rain clouds that smothered the moon and stars, was inky black. He would need to be careful where he went and avoid potential holes and bumpy paths. An injury right now was the last thing he needed. There were barely any cars and so he took the decision to run in the road. If anything did come, he'd hear it and get out the way.

Harrison started slowly, trying hard to pull his brain's focus away from all the myriad of things that were swirling around inside his head and competing for his attention. He stared at the road just ahead of his feet, concentrating on one step after another, and on keeping his eyes open and alert despite the rain smashing into his face. The run home would be easier because the wind and rain would be on his back, but for now, it felt like he was running against an invisible force.

One step after another. Gradually, he picked up speed.

Slowly his heartbeat increased and the pull on his lungs became deeper.

He tried to go faster, but his pace was ragged and he couldn't find his usual rhythm.

He pushed on, towards the end of the high street where the properties grew less dense and the darkness seemed like a black tunnel ahead of him.

There was a flash of something up ahead. It made him falter, lose his concentration. It flew across the road - probably just an owl, but it had been enough to cause him to mis-step and a pain seared through his right thigh. He limped to a walk and bent over, rubbing his leg. This was crazy. Even his running was falling apart, his muscles so tense they were prone to injury. He felt like a pent up pressure cooker, needing to let off steam and yet he had no idea how to do it or what he needed to do. Harrison rubbed hard at the muscle, warming it up, pressing deep into the tissue to take the tension out of it.

Finally, he turned and slowly jogged back to the pub. If he didn't sort himself out, then not only would he lose his own self-control, but he'd be totally useless to this investigation. The pieces were all there starting to form in front of him, and yet he felt incapable of concentrating in order to put them into any kind of clear picture. The vampires, the heart attacks, the family curse. They had to have some rational explanation and he should be able to see it, but he couldn't. Desmond Manning and the evil which followed him around were winning. The fog in his head wouldn't clear. He had to find a way out of this situation, and soon.

16

Harrison took a hot shower and pummelled his thigh muscle again so that by the time he was ready to go downstairs for dinner, it was just a slight niggle in his leg.

When he'd got back to his room, there was a text from Joe. "Sorry just heading out on a long one. Can we chat tomorrow? I have the day off."

He felt disappointment, but he replied to say no problem and that he'd call him tomorrow. Then he sat for a few moments, imagining Joe in one of the trucks, driving through the dusty terrain to a location where they'd probably had a tip off that people were running drugs across. Every week there was a new route, new couriers. The rewards were too high for impoverished people to refuse, and so the drug lords had a plentiful supply of willing recruits prepared to risk everything. Sometimes it was their own people who succumbed to the lure of the drugs money and Harrison knew Joe always found that a harder arrest to make.

Before he left the room for dinner, he did a quick check-in call with Ryan.

'Boss!'

'Ryan, how are things?'

'All good. How's the case?'

'Fine. Still early days yet. Have you got anywhere with the vampire hunt?'

'No, actually, really struggling with this one. I can't find any drama groups, vampire fetish clubs, or real life blood drinkers, who will admit to being around the area, or who even look like there was a possibility they were there.'

'Hmm, I've got them to do some extra toxicology tests. Perhaps it could have been some kind of psychosis or hallucination then. We'll see what they dig up.'

'You sure it's not the villagers? You know, like some kind of weird wicker man thing going on where a load of them gather at the stones to worship the vampire and cover it all up between them? You did say he came from the village originally.'

'It's an idea, Ryan, but I don't think so. There's no evidence of that yet.'

'Well, if I were you, I'd be eating a ton of garlic tonight. Apparently, each person's blood tastes different, so maybe if you make yourself really garlicky, they'll leave you alone.'

'Unless they happen to like garlic,' Harrison felt himself smiling at Ryan's primitive safety measures.

'Yeah, true. Perhaps it was only Dracula who didn't like it.'

Harrison wasn't entirely sure how they'd got into that conversation, but he was grateful that it had at least taken his mind off things.

. . .

There were more people in the pub when he got downstairs and he particularly noticed a group of young people sitting around one of the tables in the far corner. They reminded him of Ryan, pale-faced geeks, introverts avoiding the gaze of anybody else in the pub. Perhaps they were people who might know about local vampire groups.

Penny and Matt were still behind the bar, chatting, pulling pints, and pouring drinks. Harrison presumed Sally was in the kitchen cooking the many meals which every now and again appeared and were taken across to tables in the dining area.

'Good evening Dr Lane,' Penny said, 'here's the menu, all home-cooked, no micro-waved meals here.'

Harrison glanced at it, realising he was actually quite hungry after a day on the road. DI Christie had recommended lasagna, and that sounded like an altogether good option, but he scanned the starters, preferring something savoury as an extra course, rather than a sweet pudding afterwards.

He smiled to himself when he saw that one of the options was creamy garlic mushrooms with local rustic bread. Maybe he should follow Ryan's advice. He ordered the garlic mushrooms and lasagna along with a diet Coke. Then Harrison parked himself at the bar so that he could listen to some of the conversations going on around him, and perhaps ask a few questions of his own.

On his right were two men who looked like they were involved in farming. They had rugged complexions and calloused hands which told of an outdoor lifestyle, along with sensible clothing and footwear, which had mud caked into the soles. Both were drinking pints, although there wasn't a huge deal of conversation flowing between them. It was a different matter to the left where two couples were positioned; the girls sitting on barstools and the men standing, nursing their pints.

'Mary in the shop says her cat might have been attacked by the vampire. It was behaving oddly. Clawed her hand when she tried to stroke him and hissed at her. When she took him to the vets, they found a puncture wound on his neck that had become infected and bite marks along his back.'

'Didn't that original vampire eat cats?' The other woman joined in.

'It's probably just from a bloody cat fight,' one of the men interjected, looking to the other man for some kind of common sense back-up.

'And you know that, do you?' The first girl retorted, 'So how comes Carole Templeton saw them, you've always told me she's really smart.'

'Well... I don't know, maybe it was somebody mucking around.'

'Mucking around include running her off the cliff and killing her?'

He shrugged. 'I don't get why Richard Templeton was digging around there in the first place. Should have left things alone.'

The other man joined in the conversation now, clearly deciding that it had got too serious. 'So is Mary going to drive a stake through her cat's heart and put it out in the sun to see if it burns up?' He laughed at his own joke and his male friend joined in. The two women just glared at them.

'Your table is ready, love,' Penny's voice interrupted Harrison's listening. The two couples watched him as he got up and followed Penny over to the dining area, where she showed him a table set for one.

'The vampire story seems to have got a few people talking in the village,' Harrison said to her.

'There's a lot round here who are worried about the curse and what happened to the Templetons and the Doctor's boy. I know it might seem strange to city folk, but it's a close-knit community here, and those stories got passed down through the generations. Whatever the reason for the deaths, it isn't a good thing, and it's spooked folk.'

Penny walked off and back to the bar and in her wake, Harrison saw Matt heading towards him, bearing a bowl of creamy mushrooms and a plate with fresh crusty bread. His stomach rumbled.

The food was as good as DI Christie had promised, and he was glad he'd taken his recommendation for the lasagna. It was certainly one of the best he'd ever tasted. Once he'd finished, Harrison contemplated going straight back up to his room like he normally would, but instead he forced himself to return to the bar, still interested in hearing any other gossip and, if possible, talking to the group in the corner.

Within ten minutes, he was in luck as one of the lads in the group got up with their empty glasses and headed towards the bar for refills. By now, the two farm workers had left, no doubt because they had an early start in the morning. Harrison made sure there was a clear space for the lad to get access, and that it was right next to where he was standing.

He was a skinny young man, jet black hair with tinted glasses, the antithesis of a sporty jock. The only muscle tone on his body would be from operating a computer mouse and the winter fleece he had on probably doubled his body size, but still, he looked thin. His skin was beyond white, almost translucent, as though he never ventured outside. He put the drinks glasses on the bar and waited for Penny to finish serving another customer, angling his body slightly away from Harrison so as to avoid eye contact. It was obvious he didn't want to chat, but Harrison spoke anyway.

'You live around here?'

The lad looked a little startled and uncomfortable, but gave a small nod.

'Nice village,' Harrison continued. If it had been a normal conversation, Harrison would've got the message that the lad didn't want to talk, but this wasn't. He wanted information and so he pushed. 'I can't believe all these rumours of vampires and curses, though. You don't think there's any truth to it, do you?'

The lad looked at him now, just briefly, but long enough for him to see fear in his eyes.

'No,' he said and a second later, pushed himself off the bar and walked back to his group of friends. Harrison watched as he said something to them, and then all five of them stood up and quickly left the bar.

Penny clattered the dirty glasses together from the bar top.

'You're bad for business, you are,' she said, but in a good natured way.

'Do you know who they are, if they live around here?'

'Only seen one or two of them in here occasionally.' She called Matt over. 'Did you recognise any of that group who were sitting in the corner?'

Matt looked to where the group had been sitting.

'Yeah, I was at school with a couple of them. They were geeks, Melissa Ravenscroft and David Welsh.'

'You say geeks? Would you say they were into the goth scene or the supernatural?' Harrison asked.

'You mean vampires and stuff? I dunno, they were just nerds, but they're harmless.'

Harrison looked at the empty seats and wondered why they'd left so quickly after his question. Might just be they'd wanted to avoid drawing attention to themselves, or perhaps they did know something. He texted the two names Matt had given him to Ryan, and then retired to his room, knowing there was a kettle on the desk which was just what he needed for the chamomile tea bags he'd brought with him.

Just as he got back to the room, a text arrived from Tanya. It took him back to that morning, lying in bed with her smooth, warm body nestled against his. Her soft naked skin beneath his hands.

A warmth flowed through him, and a sigh escaped, allowing a momentary moment of relaxation. It was short-lived, quickly replaced by more anxiety. Was he doing the right thing by allowing their relationship to keep going like this? What future could he offer her? He could never give up his job. It was a lifelong quest, and that meant a lifetime on the road, travelling to wherever he was needed. Who was he even kidding? He was needed here, and he couldn't even get his head together enough to be able to help. Had he lost his ability to focus? Had the infection of his genetic father and the Mannings finally overcome him?

He longed to hear her voice, for it to curl its way into his ear and soothe his thoughts, but he didn't ring. Instead, he texted her and told her he was really tired, in bed and just going to sleep. He would speak to her tomorrow.

Tanya deserved better than him. She deserved a man with both a past and a future. Someone who was there for her, not chasing the evil of people's imaginations and beliefs, or his own ghosts.

17

Cheryl closed her bedroom door as quietly as she could, a skill she'd mastered well over the years whenever she didn't want her parents knowing she was up late. She'd been unable to sleep for the last few nights, ever since she'd heard them talking about it. Ordinarily she might have traded on the revelation at school, earned cool points with her mates, and especially those who thought her just dull Cheryl, but these weren't ordinary times. She was scared.

She read everything she could about it on the internet, but still the fear wound its way through her guts, causing her heart to hammer in her chest and the blood to whoosh into her ears.

When she lay still, she could feel it. The curse crept around her heart like ants on an iced bun, crawling across it, burrowing into her blood vessels, making her heart race and skip beats. The more she felt it, the more scared she got, and the worse it became. At night she lay in the darkness, thinking about being dead. The nothing. The end. She would cease to be. Her body would rot and disappear and the world would go on without her. It felt like she was falling into a dark endless pit of panic, a grave with such deep walls she had no way of escape. Never to see her parents again. Never to look at the world. Never to breathe again.

She'd nearly passed out in PE today, the tiredness starting to win the battle. Tonight the wind and rain conjured up the perfect storm of teenage imagination and village gossip, which whipped her into a frenzy of anxiety. Would she die in her sleep like the others? Was the curse coming for her?

18

Harrison woke up with a headache, which wasn't surprising considering the fitful sleep he'd had. He didn't have any pain killers and so he drank some water and hoped it would disappear. If it didn't, then he'd get something later.

The headache added to the cacophony of noise and confusion in his head. He'd intended to fast, but with his inability to concentrate as it was, he decided to skip the fasting and see if eating one of Sally's apparently legendary breakfasts, would help him feel better.

Down in the pub, a cleaner had just finished hoovering and wiping the tables down, and was winding up the vacuum cleaner cord ready to put it away. She watched him with half an eye, like a cat. Penny was checking the stock behind the bar. She popped her head up as Harrison walked in.

'Morning Dr Lane,' she said brightly, 'would you like a full English this morning?'

Harrison hesitated a moment and then said yes. He

probably wouldn't eat lunch and it was likely to be another long day.

'Sleep well?' Penny asked.

He knew she was hoping he'd found the room comfortable, which it was, that hadn't been his problem.

'Yes thank you,' he lied.

'Good, we've only recently had the rooms refurbished, trying to build up some more tourist trade,' she added.

'Do you get many tourists coming to the area?'

'A few. Mostly walkers, but we get people who are visiting Fountains Abbey, or to walk around Brimham Rocks before heading up to the Captain Cook memorial museum. Most view us as a stop over just for a night or two. We need to encourage longer stays.'

'Isn't there a hotel company trying to buy the Templetons' house?'

'Yes. If they do agree to sell, then it will be good for our business. Whatever promotions and advertising they do will benefit us all. We cater to a slightly different market and people.'

'Do you think the other villagers share your views?' He queried.

Penny stopped for a moment and looked at him, studying his face. Her own features had lost their friendly sparkle. He could tell she was trying to see if he had a motive behind that question.

'There's not much in the way of work around here unless you go into the city. I'm sure there'd be plenty of people who would welcome a fresh injection of tourism and its money into the area.' She finally said. 'I'm just going to let Sally know you'd like the full English.' With that, she was gone.

Harrison wondered just how much of a desire there was for the Templetons to sell up and their home to be turned into a hotel. The vicar wanted to boost his congregation, the pub its clientele, and people wanted the work. Who might resort to pressurising the family from their home and what lengths would they go to? Then there was Dr Rowland, he was trying to prevent the hotel from buying the house. Would someone resort to murdering his son in order to put him off the purchase? Every way he turned, there were potential motives and potential suspects. Was Ryan right? Was the village in on the plan, or at least some of the village? He was starting to feel a creep of paranoia and that was something totally alien to him.

The other thing that Harrison wasn't used to feeling, was that of dread when he walked back into the incident room. He'd never experienced this kind of blockage in his head before on an investigation. There were so many different elements to it and he couldn't see the pattern, or work out the whole picture. They needed the toxicology results for Carole, that would rule out or confirm a hallucination. Or was there something else going on, was someone using the stories of curses and vampires to manipulate people in order for financial gain?

Haynes barely acknowledged him when he arrived, but Lucy Robinson gave him a cheery smile.

'I need to speak to Bob Williams today,' he said as he walked up to Adam Christie's desk. 'Shall I take DC Robinson with me?'

'She's been assigned some house to house duties today, we're trying to talk to all the villagers and see if anyone noticed any strangers in the area the night of Carole's death. I appreciate Scott isn't the easiest person to be around, but he does know this neighbourhood well.'

'It's fine,' Harrison tried to sound positive.

Haynes made him wait until he'd had a cup of coffee and a large Danish Whirl. It took him a surprisingly long time to eat the pastry and with each lick of his fingers, Harrison had to quell the urge to not walk straight over to him and ram it down his throat. The man was clearly trying to show he was in control. Harrison played the pastry attack scenario over and over in his head so many times that at one point he had to walk out of the room because it was fast becoming an acceptable thing to do.

When he got back, the DS was ready. 'Wondered where you'd got to,' he said. 'Come on, Bob Williams is expecting us.'

As they walked out the room, Harrison calculated how much effort it would take to pick the man up and hurl him through the window. He'd definitely make it to the car park quicker that way.

In the car, without his audience, Haynes mellowed slightly. Being in such isolated close proximity to a man who was twice his strength, might have also had something to do with it.

'Bob's a widower. Lost his wife four or five years ago now. The house is a bit of a tip.' Mr glass half empty said to Harrison.

That was the only information he offered before they drew up to a small row of cottages just outside of the main village. At one time they'd have been farm workers' cottages, considered large enough to house a decent sized family. Nowadays the two bedrooms and downstairs bathroom, were only deemed suitable for a couple or starter family.

'Bob worked for the local paper for years. Ended up editing it, but it's only small fry stuff not like the Daily Mail. He retired to look after his wife when she became ill.'

Harrison wondered what it took to impress DS Haynes, was the vicar his only idol?

The garden was relatively neat, not the pristine precision neat of the Paulsons' yesterday, but it was a garden that clearly had some care lavished on it. A ginger cat was sat on the doorstep, twitching the end of its tail as though annoyed that they'd taken so long to arrive which meant it had to wait before the front door was opened and it could enter.

DC Haynes knocked and then stepped back and stared at the cat. The door was quickly opened by a short, balding man in a navy cardigan and corduroy trousers, both of which sported fine ginger and white hairs.

'Scott, come in,' Bob waved his hand at them both. 'Come on inside and let's get this door shut. It's cold today. Rebel, what are you waiting there for?' He spoke to the cat, which lightly tiptoed into the house ahead of them.

Bob turned and walked down the hallway, talking to them over his shoulder as he did so. 'He's got a flap in the back door but can't be bothered to walk around to get inside. You'd think in this weather he'd make the effort.'

He led them into the kitchen, where Rebel had already arrived and was tucking into something crunchy in a ceramic cat bowl.

'What can I get you both? Tea, coffee?' Bob said, waving at them to sit down around the kitchen table which had a laptop and mounds of research papers piled haphazardly on its surface.

'Coffee for me, white, one sugar,' DS Haynes was quick to put his order in.

'Just water thank you.' Harrison replied and wondered if the detective was going to introduce them.

As Bob busied himself with his hospitality task, Harrison looked around at their surroundings. The kitchen was a good size for two people; it looked as though it had been modified at some point to allow it to be a kitchen/diner with space for the table that they now sat at. The units were modern, but dated and the worktop near to the cooker scarred by a thousand knife cuts. Bob clearly wasn't into using a chopping board. On the notice board was a leaflet from the church detailing service times and contact numbers, plus a host of various tradesmen's cards: plumbers, electricians, gardeners and plasterers, plus a flyer offering 10% off your first oven clean, which clearly hadn't been cashed in.

On the windowsill was a row of plants in varying stages of their life cycle. One pot seemed to contain what had once been an orchid, but was now little more than a green twig. Another it was impossible to tell what it had once been. A mass of brown, curled leaves were all that were left to prove it had once been a living thing.

On the walls, were photographs of various scenes of the area. Harrison recognised the blood stone and its companions at sunrise, another long range view across the grounds of the Templeton house, and a moody scene of the village high street in black and white, like an image from another time.

'My wife took those. She was a keen photographer,' Bob said placing a glass of water in front of Harrison and following his eyes.

'They're very good,' Harrison replied. 'Dr Harrison Lane, I'm assisting the police with the investigation into the various unexpected deaths in the area.' Harrison put his hand out for Bob to shake it, aware they hadn't been formally introduced.

'A medical doctor? Forensics?' Bob asked.

Harrison remembered Bob had been a journalist.

'Psychologist. Head of the Ritualistic Behavioural Crime unit, to be exact.'

Bob's eyebrows went up.

'Ritualistic?' He looked to DS Haynes. 'I suppose it's the vampires that have piqued your interest,' he returned his gaze to Harrison.

'Vampires and curses, which is one of the reasons we're here. I understand you're writing a book about the area, including the various folklore.'

'Well based on recent events, I'm not so sure it is just folklore, are you?' Bob teased, but with a serious intent. He put a mug of grey liquid down in front of Haynes and sat himself down with another one.

'Can you tell us about the book first?' Harrison asked.

'Sure. I'd always wanted to write a book about the area, there's so much hidden history here, and you know as you get older you become more concerned that it will disappear and future generations won't have the stories handed down to them. I wasn't sure if I was going to just self-publish it locally, but in the end, I approached a publisher with the idea and they really liked it. Well to be exact, they really like certain elements of it. The Templeton family curse, the vampire and the blood stone. Since the tragic events in the last two weeks, they've even managed to secure a national newspaper serialisation deal. It will be a pretty big dose of publicity for our little village.'

Bob's face shone with smug pride and excitement.

'Have you had much support or opposition to the book?'

'Oh lots of support, most people are keen to put the place on the map.'

'People except for Richard Templeton? I understand you're including a history of the Templeton family and he wasn't happy about that?'

'You're referring to our little discussion at the autumn fair?'

'Heated argument was the way it was described.'

Bob shrugged.

'Richard was being a bit sensitive that's all. It's not like I was going to write anything that wasn't common knowledge in the village.' He looked from Haynes to Harrison. 'Seriously. I mean Scott, you know all the stories, everyone does.'

'Can you tell me?' Harrison asked calmly.

'OK, so Henry Templeton fancied himself as a bit of an adventurer. He paid two of the young men in the village to go with him on one of his hair-brained trips to Malaysia and got them both killed. That's the basis of the curse story. Henry took some items from what he thought was an abandoned temple and the local tribe didn't take too kindly to it. He was lucky to get out alive, of course the hired help weren't quite so fortunate. He paid the families off and thought that would be the end of it.'

'So why did Henry think he'd been cursed? I know the two men died in Malaysia, but that wouldn't necessarily have been that unusual in those days with malaria and other diseases in tropical locations, not to mention unfriendly locals.' Harrison asked.

'No, quite right and I don't think Henry was overly bothered about them, not until he started to believe that the tribe he'd taken things from, had indeed cursed his family. They'd been warned apparently that anyone trespassing in the temple would be cursed, and while Henry got out alive, his brother wasn't so lucky.'

'His brother?' DS Haynes interrupted, surprised. 'Never knew he had one.'

'Yes, Edward Templeton is somebody that the

Templetons don't mention. It was one of the things Richard was sensitive about, the family had always tried to keep that side of it quiet. Edward Templeton was Henry's younger brother. Bright young man by all accounts, preferred to have his head in books rather than parading around as the big brave adventurer like his brother. They were very different, but Henry doted on him. Rumour was he'd been the brains behind their business ventures and from what I can find in the records, I think that was probably true. Edward stayed at home, but shortly after Henry returned from Malaysia, he died in somewhat mysterious circumstances. Obviously it's hard to get a clear idea of what killed him, but cause of death was put down as angina pectoris as a result of mental strain and excitement, what we would call a heart attack. They believed that diseases of the heart were closely linked to the psyche and emotions in those days, which I suppose has some truth but is likely to have only been half the story. I think that Edward was most likely gay. If you look at all the paintings of him, the things that have been said about his effeminate character and mannerisms, and the depression he suffered from, plus the way he isolated himself from society, I'd say that's what the evidence points to. It wasn't easy being a gay man in those days, he'd have felt tremendous pressure to marry and produce, but probably just couldn't bring himself to do so, he was unmarried at his death and there'd been scant talk of potential suitors. Anyway, poor Edward had been seeing a physician prior to his death, who reported he was anxious following his brother's return and had a fear of impending death. Alas for him, he was right. After that, Henry declared that the family was cursed and buried whatever it was he brought back from Malaysia underneath the blood stone, much to the disgust of the curate at the time. To appease all possible deities, he also invested heavily in the village church, hoping to ensure he covered all bases, nullified the curse and bought his brother a passage to heaven. Henry was devastated by all accounts, and forbid anyone mentioning Edward's name ever again, and decreed that all paintings of him should be taken down. Now whether that was because he was genuinely upset and loved his brother, or because he was angry at losing his business partner, is anyone's guess.'

Bob paused a moment, taking a big long sip of his coffee for dramatic effect.

'The other issue, is that Henry Templeton wasn't just an adventurer overseas. He liked to venture into the village and visit any pretty young women there too. John Rowland's grandfather was one of the two men who died on that ill fated Malaysian trip. Thing was, his wife wasn't pregnant when he left, and John's father wasn't born until over a year after Henry Templeton returned. John's grandfather wasn't the man who died in Malaysia, he was Henry Templeton, which makes both Richard and John his grandsons.'

'Does John know that?' Harrison asked.

'Oh yes. It's the main reason why he really wants to buy the estate. He isn't the only one though. There are a few others in the village who can owe their bloodline to the Templetons. Henry was free with his affections.'

'This is all history though, so why would Richard be upset about people knowing this, if those involved already knew, anyway?'

Bob shrugged again.

'In my view, I think Richard liked a quiet life. He was afraid it would bring people flocking to his house and to his land. He also wasn't keen on our Reverend Davenport, who I have to say was surprisingly excited about the prospect of the vampire story bringing new interest in his church.'

'Why wasn't Richard keen on the reverend?'

'Have you met Brian? He's a full on fire and brimstone traditionalist, some might say his views are very outdated and not politically correct. Richard tolerated him, just, but when he got quite animated about the book and the possible positives for his church, Richard saw red. If I'm honest, and Scott please don't quote me on this, I thought it a bit hypocritical that someone who preaches the merits of Christianity, was so keen on spreading pagan stories in order to increase his congregation.'

Bob was in full swing and clearly enjoying spreading his gossip, but Harrison saw DS Haynes bristle and spoke quickly to diffuse the situation. He didn't want Bob clamming up if the detective got annoyed.

'He's a bit of a marmite man then, the Reverend Davenport,' Harrison stated, rather than asking the question. 'How did the conversation between the three of you end?'

'Margaret came up to speak to Richard. I think she'd seen him getting angry and must have decided to try to calm things down and see what was going on.'

Harrison nodded thoughtfully. 'I understand you edited the local paper for a long time.'

'Yes, still do the odd article for them.'

'Did you ever write any stories about people around here dressing up as vampires and going to the stones, or there being any kind of underground scene?'

Bob shook his head emphatically.

'No. I don't know what poor Carole saw that day, but it's certainly not something anyone has ever reported before. We've had our share of crop circles and alien sightings, we even had someone who claimed to have been possessed by a witch, but the vampire story has lain dormant for years.'

'Reverend Davenport showed us the ledger in which the story was originally recorded by the curate at the time. He said he'd shown it to you.'

'That's correct.'

'Was this before or after the autumn fair?'

'After. He called me the next day and said he'd found the original records. Must have been up half the night searching through those dusty old books. I told you he was keen.'

19

For a few minutes, Ryan sat staring at his computer screen as the weight of the knowledge he now held sunk in. What now? The finding him had been the easy part, the next bit was the tough one. Morally, he should hand the information over instantly to the detective leading the murder inquiry, Inspector Gordon Jacobsen. His loyalty, however, was to Harrison and he knew that there were questions he had for Desmond Manning which wouldn't get answered in a police interview room. The issue was, would Harrison stop at just questions, or would the years of anger born out of trying to prove his mother's death wasn't suicide, and that Desmond may well have been her killer, result in Harrison killing him himself? He couldn't risk that. He couldn't put his boss in a position where he might not be able to control himself. So what should he do?

The task was made all the harder by the fact Harrison was about two-hundred and fifty miles away. Communicating with him was only possible via the phone and internet, in situations like this, he needed to see his face and judge the look in his eyes.

He tried to think what Harrison himself would do if he was faced with such a decision. He had a strong moral code, but he understood that lines were sometimes fluid and every situation was unique. This situation was certainly unique!

Ryan opened another can of coke and finished off the pack of giant Wotsits, which he'd opened the day before. It would do for his breakfast. After an hour's deep thinking, he realised there really was only one option, but he would have to get the timing absolutely right if it was to succeed. He was also going to need some help along with precision planning.

20

Talking to Bob Williams had been useful, but it seemed to open up more questions rather than give answers. When they got back to the incident room and DI Christie called for a briefing with the whole team, Harrison's heart sank. He had no answers for them yet. No clear idea of the motivations behind what was going on. Were they even connected? Had a crime been committed?

'We've got the toxicology back on Carole,' Adam began, 'No sign of any hallucinants or drugs.'

The team around the table all sighed as another potential route through the maze was closed off. Harrison could feel their frustration.

'In your professional view, could she have imagined those vampires?' The DI asked him.

'I don't think so. If she was having some kind of psychotic episode, there'd have been a build-up, some other evidence of it. She appears too calm and rational when she starts the phone call to her mother. You can hear in her voice and in her breathing when she sees them.' Harrison said the words, but his confidence was wavering. Was his judgement as good as it should be? 'I would just like to confirm that it wasn't a form of psychosis by speaking to the florist and anyone else who might have spoken to her that day before she went to the stones, but her medical history indicates no psychological issues at all, not even stress. You would expect to see some other hallucinations and some cognitive impairment, but she'd been at work until just a few days before with no issues. In my view, she definitely saw something that day. The question is, did the association with the legend and the place, make her mind believe she was seeing something that was in fact quite different.'

'What do you mean? How's that different to a hallucination?'

'I mean, that they were real. But, was it a group of people, perhaps dressed for an event, a night out or something, who'd stopped off to watch the sunset at the stones? However, because she was upset, had been thinking about the curse and by default, the vampire story, did she then interpret what she saw incorrectly?'

'So why didn't they call 999 when she went off the cliff?' DC Robinson asked.

'Because they were worried they might get blamed. Or, maybe they weren't supposed to be there.' Sergeant Cutter answered. 'You'd be surprised how many people will turn the other cheek.'

'So it was just an accident?' Lucy asked the room.

'Maybe, or maybe not. Until we've tracked down whoever was there that evening, we're not going to get an answer.' Christie answered.

'I spoke to as many people as I could this morning. None of them saw anybody or anything unusual that day. There are no reports of any strangers in the village. I stopped at the pub and Sally and Penny said the place was pretty empty, just a couple of regulars.' She added.

'Perhaps they weren't strangers, maybe it's people who live here,' Harrison mused out loud.

The rest of the team looked at him.

'I'm going to put out another media appeal, see if we can persuade whoever it was there that night, to come forward. Surely someone in the group must have a conscience.' Christie replied and sighed. 'OK, so let's park Carole and look at the heart attacks. We've got Richard, Jasper, and Lee Rowland. None of whom appear to have had any heart issues. In fact, we categorically know that Richard didn't because he'd had the health check. Any updates?'

'We've just been with Bob Williams. There's a definite link between Lee and the Templetons, in fact they're related.' Haynes leaned back in his chair, enjoying being the bearer of potentially critical information. 'Henry Templeton, he who started the curse, was his great grandfather. Plus, he isn't the only one. There are others in the village who were illegitimate offspring.'

DI Christie sat upright and put his elbows on the table, eyes narrowed, wanting more.

'Did John know this?'

'Yes, it's not a secret apparently, and it's one of the reasons why John is so keen to buy the Templeton estate.'

The DI thought for a few moments. 'So, how could that fit with a motive for murder?'

There was silence for a few moments as the whole room thought through the puzzle.

'It doesn't make sense still does it boss?' Lucy spoke now, frowning. 'If John Rowland wanted to clear the way for him and his son to get the estate, then why is Lee dead? Why else would anyone want to kill the Templeton bloodline unless they absolutely hated them, but it's a bit drastic isn't it?'

'There are a couple of other possible motivations,' Harrison spoke now. 'A hotel group is trying to buy the Templeton estate and there are quite a few in the village who would welcome the prosperity that would bring. Money is a drastic motivator for some and Richard didn't want to sell.'

'But why Lee then?'

'As we've said, John Rowland wanted to buy the estate instead, he offered more. He'd have kept it as a private house.'

'You said a couple of motivations?'

'The book that Bob is writing could bring tourists to the area too, that would benefit the same people. Since this all kicked off, the publishers have secured a major national newspaper serialisation deal, it's been good for publicity, to put it mildly.'

'So potential suspects include Bob, and any of those who want to see a boost in tourism? Well, that's at least half the village then!'

'That's if any of the deaths are actually connected.' Harrison threw the last bombshell. 'We could still be looking for a pattern when it's really just a series of random events.'

'Or it could be an ancient curse striking down the Templeton bloodline,' Adam Christie threw his hands up in exasperation. 'In truth, we're no closer to knowing, are we? We still have a series of unexplained deaths, a host of potential suspects and motives, but no definite idea if these people were murdered or just unlucky. I've got every newspaper in the land knocking on my door wanting to know if we're calling in an exorcist or some kind of demon hunter to track down these vampires and appease the curse. Did you see the interview on Breakfast TV this morning?' He asked the whole room, but didn't wait for their answers. 'They had a serious discussion about whether some ancient race of vampires could realistically be living amongst us and have been woken up in our village. I mean really?'

Harrison felt the DI's frustration. They all did, but he felt it more keenly. He was the specialist called in to dispel the curse and vampire rumours and work out what was really going on, but he couldn't. There was something, tantalisingly there at the back of his mind which could provide an answer, but he couldn't grasp it.

THE FRUSTRATING MEETING turned into a frustrating afternoon.

Harrison went into the village to visit the florists and find out if anyone else had seen Carole Templeton the day she died. It was also a good excuse to go and take a look around, get a better feel for the place.

The village shops, were not surprisingly, overwhelmed with Christmas cheer. Signs advertised the perfect gifts and buy now, delivery before Christmas. Colourful foil decorations and flashing lights were in every window, and there were plenty of shoppers out, their hands full of bulging carrier bags.

The florists were in full Christmas table centrepiece mode. Two women were working with green oasis foam, jabbing silver and gold sprayed twigs, holly, pine cones, green ferns and berries around white candles.

'Good afternoon, how can we help?' The older lady smiled broadly at Harrison, without stopping her oasis foam stabbing.

'I'm working with the police,' Harrison began, fishing his ID out of his pocket, and I understand that Carole Templeton came into your shop to get some flowers for her father on the day she died.

Both of their faces changed at the mention of Carole.

'So tragic,' the older woman said, shaking her head. 'So young. Yes, she came in for a small bouquet. Her father liked roses and so we made her a nice selection up.'

'How was she?'

'Well, as you'd expect. Quiet, clearly very upset about her father.'

'Calm and rational?'

'Absolutely. Not someone who looked like they would imagine a group of vampires or drive themselves off a cliff, if that's what you mean.'

Harrison nodded. 'I don't suppose you know if she went straight to the stones from your shop, or if she went anywhere else after?'

'Well, I can't say for sure, but she said she was going straight there because it was going to get dark fairly soon.'

'OK, thank you for your help.'

That all made sense. He knew that no other shopping was found in Carole's car, so if she had been anywhere else, it wasn't to buy anything. He left the women to their festive flower arranging and stepped back out into the street. A little way up the road was a bank with a cashpoint. They might have CCTV he could view, but what would it show? He was interested in what was going on inside her head, and if the vicar and the florist said she was upset but calm and rational, then she wasn't exhibiting any physical signs of psychosis.

Just in case she'd bumped into somebody who upset her, Harrison asked in a couple of other shops. Only one person remembered seeing her that day and mentioned she was on her own carrying a bunch of flowers. The likelihood she went straight to the stones after buying the bouquet, increased. It was frustrating; he was getting nowhere.

Eventually, Harrison found himself back at the Druid's Arms. His headache had returned with a vengeance and so he returned to his room to close his eyes and lie down. He felt like not only his concentration and confidence were slipping away, but so too was his strength. After taking some paracetamol and resting for half an hour, he called Arizona.

Hearing Joe pick up, no matter how far away he was, made him feel as though a comfort blanket had been thrown around him. It took Joe seconds to realise that something was wrong. Harrison filled him in on the events involving the Mannings, and the revelation as to who his genetic father was.

'I had no idea,' Joe said.

Harrison heard the sadness in his voice.

'Why didn't she tell us? How could she have chosen a man like that?'

'Good people make mistakes. Evil people manipulate and fool the best of us with their lies. You of all people should understand that, it's the key to what you do every day.'

Harrison knew it was true, but it was easier to see it when it wasn't so close to home.

'Perhaps she also felt ashamed.' Joe continued. 'Perhaps most of all she didn't want you to think less of her and for her shame to be yours. If she kept that part of your lives away from you then it couldn't touch you.'

The emotions of the past 48 hours came pouring out of Harrison and he surprised even himself with the words that came from his mouth. He'd not realised just how much the revelations about this genetic father had impacted him.

'I've got no idea who she was anymore. The woman I thought I knew has been wiped out by this. I'm not sure I know how to forgive her.'

Joe sighed sadly.

'She is still the mother you remember. There is one thing I do know, and that is your mother was not a bad person. Do you think we would have stayed together so long if she had been? She had a good soul.'

'Then why did she take us back to the UK? Why didn't we just stay with you where we were both safe?'

'You know I don't have the answer to that question. She told me that she had to return but never why.'

'If she realised what kind of man my father was, did she look at me every day and regret I even existed? Did she see his features in me, his anger in mine? I feel like I've not just lost sight of her, I've lost sight of myself.'

' No.' Joe's voice came to him strong and hard. 'She loved you more than anything in the world. You are not that man your genetic father is. Everything you have done with your life defines you and differentiates you from him. Your mother would have been so proud of you and that's who you are, not a string of letters in a DNA sequence.'

Harrison's throat was tight with holding back his emotions. He'd have given anything to be in the same room as Joe, to see his wise eyes and feel enveloped in his embrace.

'You must find yourself again.' Joe continued. 'When my people were taken from their lands and stripped of their culture, forbidden to follow the traditions and practices our forefathers had followed for centuries, some lost sight of themselves. Their minds became black, and they turned to drink and to drugs to forget their feeling of worthlessness. It fed on the depression in their soul and so it destroyed them. Suicides, ill health, addictions, they were all the symptoms of a lost soul. You must find yourself again. The man who you created. You alone. You forged your way through your mother's love and your own strength. You have to find that path again.'

21

Ryan had stared at his handset for a moment too long, as Harrison's name flashed at him. He was a little nervous about picking up the phone to his boss, he'd never been a good liar and he wasn't yet ready to tell him he'd tracked down Desmond Manning.

Ryan couldn't ignore the call though, Harrison was razor sharp and would know something was up.

'Boss!'

'Ryan, how are things?'

'Fine.'

There was a slight pause as Harrison expected Ryan to continue chatting like he usually would, but he didn't.

'Any news?' Harrison pushed.

'No. All quiet here. I'm still hunting the vampires but it's slow progress.'

'Did you track down the two names I'd given you?'

'Not yet, working on it, but they don't seem to have much of a social presence - well actually no social presence. What was it about them that made them stand out to you?'

'They reminded me of you at first, pale introverts, you

know the type,' Harrison said half jokingly, 'spend their lives in dark rooms.'

'Are you suggesting that I'm a vampire?' Ryan asked.

'Not unless vampires drink Coke and prefer nachos to necks. No.'

Ryan smiled down the phone. 'I'll keep looking, I'm sure I'll come up with some inspiration.'

Harrison was grateful that at least one of them was still able to come up with ideas.

'Thanks Ryan.' Harrison replied, but when he'd ended the phone call without Ryan mentioning the hunt for Desmond Manning, he knew that his assistant was holding back. The question was, why and how should he handle it.

Ryan, on his part, thought he'd got away with it.

DESPITE FEELING TIRED, sleep wouldn't come to Harrison. Every time he closed his eyes a jumble of images leered out at him. Vampires chasing Carole Templeton off the cliff, a young lad lying dead in his bed, Richard digging around the blood stone searching for something, but what did he take out of the hole that day? Had there been a treasure which someone was prepared to kill for? Then in the background of all this, leered Desmond Manning and the shadowed spectre of the man he now knew to be his genetic father. When would he have closure on any of this?

Eventually at 2am he texted Ryan.

'If you find Manning please tell me asap. Need closure.'

He hadn't wanted to accuse him directly of withholding information; he trusted him, but he also knew it would prick Ryan's conscience if he had found him.

Finally at about 3am, he fell asleep to the sound of the

rain hammering at his window again like the incessant thoughts and doubts which refused to leave his head.

RYAN PICKED up Harrison's text at 2 am but he didn't respond. He'd worked out all the timings and had everything else prepared. He wasn't going to make Harrison wait much longer, even if it did mean interrupting his investigation, but he'd had to be sure that all bases were covered.

WHEN HARRISON WOKE up the next morning, the first thing he noticed was that the rain has stopped. It was quiet both in the pub, and outside in the street and it was still dark, the winter sun not yet showing its pale face. As soon as he became fully conscious, he grabbed his mobile phone to see if Ryan had replied. He had. "I've found him" the words made Harrison's heart jump into his throat. Ryan had sent him an address which was on the Welsh borders. Harrison shot up out of bed, did some quick route calculations and then threw on some clothes and headed straight for his bike. He sent a short text to DI Christie telling him that an emergency had come up and he'd be back in tomorrow. Getting to that address was now his only priority. He needed to reach Desmond Manning before anyone else, and get the answers to the questions which had plagued him for years.

22

Harrison rode hard all the way. He'd seen Desmond Manning only once since his mother's death, that brief appearance at Nunhead cemetery, when Freda and Desmond had taunted him. Harrison had become successful at investigating and stopping people like the Mannings, they'd been both his nemesis and his driving force. Exposing people like them, who traded in false beliefs and took advantage of the vulnerable, had become his life's work. Finally, he was going to have the opportunity to bring the catalyst of all the pain in his life, to justice.

When Harrison arrived at the address Ryan had given him, it was just gone 10am and he'd only stopped to fill up on petrol and down a coffee. He parked his bike further down the street, aware that the engine could warn Desmond of his arrival. As he got off his bike, he felt the stiffness in his arms and shoulders and realised he'd been holding hard onto the handlebars, gripping far tighter than he needed to. He rubbed his hands and rolled his shoulders, and forced himself to stand a moment to gather his concentration.

There could be no room for mistakes. He'd waited years for this moment, he had to make sure he got the job done.

The first thing Harrison did, was to recce the property. It was a dive with scruffy curtains that looked like they'd been hanging in the windows for decades, not just years, and the garden was a jumble of weeds and rubbish. The front door looked like it had been broken into once already, there was damage and evidence of a new lock, and one of the windows in the downstairs had been broken at some point and a board put up until the pane could be replaced.

Harrison could just walk right up to the front door and knock, but if Desmond was being careful - which he suspected he would be - then he'd check to see who was at the door and seeing him he'd try to escape. Smashing the front door down would be easy too, the wood looked like it would just splinter, but it would also draw a great deal of attention. There were neighbours on both sides, and directly across the street. Someone would call the police.

Instead, Harrison spotted a narrow alley between two rickety wooden fences, two doors along. He guessed it would lead to the gardens behind, and that would be his best bet to gain entry.

Keeping close to the inside of the path, so as to avoid Desmond being able to see him approaching, Harrison walked to the alley and ducked straight down it. Towards the end, he could hear children playing in one of the gardens that ran alongside it, and he kept his eyes open for any possibility that he'd been spotted.

His guess had been right, and at the end, he was able to turn left or right to walk along the back of the gardens in the row of terraced houses. Desmond's was on the left.

Harrison gently tried the back gate and found it locked. There was no key access, so he surmised it was most probably just a bolt which had been shot across to close it. The fence was broken in places, enough to give him a view of the messy back garden and the rear of the house. There was no life in the windows, and nobody was looking out of the neighbouring house windows, and so he was able to reach his arm in and feel the back of the gate to see what was keeping it closed.

He found the bolt and with one last double check that nobody was watching, he gave it a bit of a wiggle and pulled it across. The gate opened easily after that, but Harrison kept it shut until he'd taken another look to ensure Desmond wasn't able to see him.

In the back garden, was a broken down shed, only small, but it would give him enough cover if he slipped in through the gate and hid behind it while he worked out how to get into the house.

After one more scan of the windows, he pushed the gate open, slipping the bolt back quickly into place, and shot across the short distance to stand behind the remains of the shed.

It was an excellent vantage spot. Here he was invisible to the neighbours, and most importantly, he had a direct view into Desmond's living room on one side, and the kitchen on the other. At first look, the house looked dark and empty, but with his closer position, Harrison could see a faint flickering of light at the far end of the living room. It was a TV, but it was mostly silhouetted by the outline of an armchair and the head of a man, sitting and watching it, facing the front street.

Harrison paused a moment, his breathing was short and shallow, and he could feel his heart pounding in his chest. It was understandable, given what he was doing, but he needed to calm himself. He couldn't afford to slip up.

For a few moments, he leaned against the shed and focused on calming his breathing. An image of his mother's face appeared in his mind. The image was of her in the photograph he had, her in a flowing flowery dress, her long blond hair flying behind her, and she was laughing and dancing. He had no idea when that picture had been taken and by who. From the background he knew it wasn't Arizona, and almost certainly the UK, but where was he, and where was his mother? She was about the same age as he was now which meant she was only a year or two from her death. He tried to feel her presence with him as he was finally within grasp of avenging her, but he felt nothing. He mourned not just her death, but the passing of time which stole away his memories of her. He could no longer hear her voice, and the image of her face was only clear from that photograph. The scraps of her he retained in his memory were just that, scraps. Grey will-o'-the-wisp glimpses without real form or shape. He tried hard to grasp at them, pull her to him. The time had come. This was for her, but she was slipping away.

Harrison turned back to take another look at the house. He had to find a way in, but when he looked, the head in the armchair had gone. All Harrison's work in calming himself became pointless as his heart leapt again. Where was Desmond? His eyes darted from window to window, and then he found him. A shadow moving in the kitchen window. He hadn't spotted Harrison; he was doing something, perhaps making a cup of tea or getting a late breakfast. A minute later, he saw the shadow cross the living room again and settle back into the chair in front of the TV.

The downstairs windows were firmly closed. They looked like they might have locks on. He would also bet that the back door was locked too. There was a pane of glass in it, which he could almost certainly smash, it wasn't reinforced, but inevitably that would make a noise and Desmond would have enough time to get out the front door before he got to him.

Harrison turned his attention to the upstairs. One of the bedroom windows was slightly ajar, and it was large enough that he would easily be able to fit through. The width of the opening told him there was no lock on it. This was his opportunity. It was above the kitchen window, so if Desmond stayed in the sitting room, it was feasible that he could climb up and get in that way without him noticing. Question was, how would he be able to reach it? He was tall, but not that tall, and even with a run up, he doubted he'd be able to jump that high.

The drain pipe ran up the wall close by, but Harrison knew his own weight and he doubted it would hold him. Even from here he could see that the brackets holding the drainpipe in place, were loose. It would collapse in a second if he tried to climb it. What he needed was something that could give him three or four extra feet in height.

Harrison turned his attention to the garden. It was much like the front, weeds mostly, intermittently interrupted by a blast of colour from rubbish: a deflated ball, a plastic chair with only three legs, or discarded carrier bags. There was certainly nothing of substance which would help him. His last hope was the shed. Would there be anything of use in there? If not, he was going to have to scour the neighbours' gardens and that meant increasing the risk of being spotted.

Checking that the coast was clear, Harrison slipped inside the small shed. The floor was rotten and his foot went through it, but it didn't hurt. He still had on his protective motorbike boots and leathers. There was no handy ladder, but there was a metal bin. It looked like it had been used for burning rubbish. It was steel, blackened but still strong. He would have to pull himself up from a hanging position, but that was fine, he knew he had the strength to do that. All he needed to do was get him and the bin across the garden to underneath that window without alerting Desmond.

Carefully, he picked up the bin and its lid; he turned the lid inside out and put it on top to increase the area he could use to help balance himself. Then he crept to the edge of the shed and peered out at Desmond's sitting-room window. The silhouette was still there. A quick glance at the neighbours, and Harrison made a dash across the garden, putting the bin against the wall of the house on the broken concrete paving, as quietly as he could.

Harrison wasn't sure if it was the noise, or perhaps Desmond saw the movement of his shadow reflected somehow, but he heard the sound of the TV pause and realised that Desmond had stood up and come to look out at the back garden. He flattened himself against the wall.

He could vaguely make out a shadowy reflection at the windowpane, but he couldn't see him which meant Desmond wouldn't be able to see him either. He hoped.

His breath was rapid and shallow, flattened against the wall, all muscles tensed. If he saw him, then he'd have to act really fast. Break through a window, catch him before he could get away. Scenarios whirred around his head. He could dive through the sitting-room window, that would be fastest. He had his leathers on so they'd protect him, or smash the back door window. That would be slower because he'd need to reach in and open the lock, presuming that it would be easy to do so, and then open the door. He decided on the window dive, but then he heard the TV volume go back on and a grunt as Desmond settled back into his armchair. Back to plan A.

For a man of his size, Harrison was very agile. Strength gave him choices that for most people would never have been an option. He hopped onto the top of the bin and steadied himself. The windowsill was a good few inches out of the reach of his fingertips. He hadn't come this far to fail now.

Centring his weight and flexing his powerful leg muscles, Harrison readied himself to jump. He had to avoid kicking the bin away because the noise of its metallic clatter would be sure to warn Desmond. The question was, would it be possible to jump up and avoid it?

He counted himself down. Every fibre in his body was on fire, the adrenaline was coursing through him, pumping his muscles full of blood and energy.

Three... two... one.

He jumped.

His fingers found the windowsill and his hands quickly grasped and held on.

Below him, the bin wobbled, a gyrating ring of metallic alarm, and then it went over.

This was it. He now had seconds.

As Desmond rushed back to the rear window to see what the noise was, Harrison used his powerful biceps and shoulder muscles to lift his weight towards the bedroom window, his feet scrabbling at the brick to give some extra push.

He was up and through the window, knocking a glass vase to the floor with a thud. That didn't matter now.

Harrison burst out of the bedroom, not looking at his surroundings and headed straight for the stairs. He could hear Desmond's feet and panicked breathing as he ran up the hallway, and he nearly fell as he rushed down the narrow steps to stop him from reaching the front door. The back of the old man's head came into view and Harrison leapt the last few stairs, landing just behind Desmond, who had bent down to grab a holdall sitting in the hallway, his grab and flight bag.

Desmond was no match for the power of Harrison. Two steps and he was on him.

He grabbed the scruff of his dressing gown and yanked him away from the door, throwing him hard against the hallway wall. A grunt of air was forced from his lungs.

'I don't think so.' Harrison growled into the old man's terrified, white face. 'It's time we had a chat.'

23

DI Jack Salter lay in bed listening to the twin sounds of breathing from those he loved. There was his wife, Marie, lying in the bed next to him, curled on her side and facing away so he could just hear her soft breathing. Then there was the little snuffly sounds, amplified by the baby monitor, which told him their son Daniel was still asleep in his cot. It was the perfect duet to wake up to, only this morning, it had been a nagging fear which had raised him from sleep and brought their sounds to his conscious ears.

Last night, he'd come home from what had been an OK day at work for him. No murders or vicious attacks, he'd been wrapping up a longstanding case, sorting through the paperwork with the prosecution service and today was going to be much of the same. Last night though, he knew something was up the moment he'd got home. Marie had already put Daniel to bed and some gentle piano music was playing in the kitchen, accompanied by his night time chatter on the baby monitor. The words weren't yet intelligible, but Jack could tell he was happily talking himself to sleep watching the mobile above his cot as it slowly spun, throwing magical little stars around his room.

He wasn't back late and Marie always kept Daniel up to say goodnight, so that was the first sign something was up. The second, was the sight of their small table in the sitting room, set up for dinner for two, with a bottle of red wine and one glass. He was a police detective; it took him seconds to scan the kitchen worktops and realise that Marie was drinking sparkling water, and to put two and two together.

'You're pregnant,' Jack blurted out as he walked into the kitchen.

Marie's face had been halfway to a smile of hello, but on seeing his reaction, hers dropped as well.

'Yes.'

A few seconds passed before either of them spoke again.

'I'm happy about it Jack. It's the right time and I know this one will be different. I'll make sure of it.'

Jack's heart and mind had exploded into two. One half of each overjoyed by the news, the other half terrified by it. Earlier that year, Marie's post natal depression had been at a crisis point. Each day that Jack had left her to go into work, he'd been on tenterhooks. She'd refused help, refused her parents visiting, and nothing he did seemed to help. Harrison had been the catalyst for change. He'd insisted that Jack come up to Norfolk with him for a case, and that he suggest to Marie she join him so that she could show her parents their new grandson. It broke the spiral of depression she'd fallen into after a traumatic birth, and she had finally sought the help that she needed.

He loved Daniel, he would love for him to have a brother or sister, but he also loved his wife and he couldn't take watching her go through that again.

'I promise I will continue to see the counsellor

throughout the pregnancy and after. I've worked through so much of the issues with Jackie. She thinks I'm ready, and she said she's happy to talk to you if you're worried.'

'So did you plan this?'

Marie shook her head.

'No. I wouldn't have planned it without talking to you first. I screwed up my contraceptive patch. I thought I'd put a new one on, was convinced I had, and by the time I realised I'd made a mistake, it must have been too late.'

Marie walked towards Jack who was still stood stock-still in the middle of their kitchen, and reached for his hands.

'I was shocked, I'll admit I was scared at first, but then I realised that our baby was growing inside of me and relying on me to take care of it. That took over. I talked it through with Jackie and she gave me the confidence to tell you. I know what I put you through last time, but it won't happen again.'

Jack looked at his wife's pleading face, he could still see the shame that had followed her recovery.

'Marie, you didn't put me through anything. It wasn't your fault, you were ill. You know I don't blame you and you know I'm 100 percent behind you. It's a shock, and I'll admit that it scares me too. I don't want to see you have to go through that again. It broke my heart watching you and being unable to help or break through.'

Tears welled in Marie's eyes.

'I know,' she said softly, 'but it won't happen like that again. I'm going to be monitored really closely so I won't be able to avoid getting support. We'll get through this without any problems and Daniel will have a brother or sister to take through life with him.'

. . .

JACK THOUGHT through their conversation as he lay in bed. It did scare him, but the ball was rolling now, there was only one way forward and that meant supporting Marie with her decision and growing their family. When Harrison was back, he'd talk to him about it. As one of the most intuitive psychologists he knew, he'd have some good advice.

Jack rolled over and looked towards the bedside table. It was early, but he wondered if something else had woken him. He reached out and picked up his phone. There was a text from Ryan.

He'd always had Ryan down as being a bit disorganised. His desk under its mound of food wrappers, bore witness to what he thought was an internet mind which couldn't focus but jumped from one thing to another without method. He knew Harrison put great store in his research capabilities, but it had always been a mystery to him. The text he read from him on his phone that morning, with the clear instructions, finely timed, and finely planned, made him realise just how organised and smart he really was. Jack replied to him immediately to say he'd read the text and understood, and within half an hour he had showered, dressed, and was heading out of his front door.

On his way out, he left a hastily drawn note to Marie, a love heart with two large stick people and two small ones inside and the message, "See you later, love you".

24

Charlotte had lain awake for what seemed to be all night. Each time she'd slipped into sleep, she'd woken up again with a terrific lurch, panic in her chest and fear in her mind.

She knew it was just a matter of time. Before long the curse would claim her, and she'd be gone. Should she speak to her parents? Tell them she knew and that the curse was true?

When her mother came in to wake her for school, she made her mind up.

'Come on Charlie, you're going to be late.' Her mother swept into the room, turning on the bedside lamp and preparing to exit in a flurry of dressing gown and towel.

'I'm not feeling too well mum. My tummy hurts and I was up in the night being sick.'

Her mother stopped and came back to look at her.

'You do look pasty and school won't want you in if you've been sick. Are you going to be OK at home on your own? Daddy and I need to get to work. I've got a big client in today so I can't work from home.'

'I'll be fine,' she'd weakly smiled at her mother. 'I just need to sleep.'

'OK then, I'll call school when I get into the office. If you need anything, then call me. I'll give you a ring about lunchtime to check you're OK.'

She heard them banging around, the clatter of breakfast, the bathroom rituals, and finally the front door closing and the car engine disappearing down the road. Then there was silence.

Charlotte's eyes slowly flickered closed.

25

DI Adam Christie woke up after only four hours of sleep having had a late night. He'd received a call at just gone 9pm the previous evening, to say Margaret Templeton had collapsed and she was being blue lighted to the nearest A and E. The first responder on the scene told him that there'd been two other people in the house at the time she fell ill. Her sister, Ciara O'Donoghue, and the Reverend Brian Davenport.

Adam's heart had plummeted when he heard the news. Had the murderer got to the last member of the Templeton family, despite their efforts? He'd immediately rung the family liaison to find out what had happened and why nobody was there keeping an eye on her.

For the next five minutes there was what could only be described as an exasperating discussion where the family liaison explained that she'd needed to go home to sort some things out before she stayed the night, and so when the Reverend Davenport turned up to comfort Margaret Templeton, she'd assumed they were in safe hands and had 'popped out', as she put it. Adam's lecture on how not to trust anybody in a murder enquiry got so heated and loud, that his wife had to come in and ask him to lower the volume because he was waking up the kids.

'I'm sorry Sir, I needed to deal with something at home.'

'And you didn't think to notify a colleague of that fact? Tell me so I could get some backup?'

'I thought it would be OK, just an hour. The Reverend and her sister were there.'

'Who was it that suggested you go? Was it your idea?'

'Err no. Now you come to mention it, I think it was the Reverend.'

By the time he'd assigned a new family liaison, and instructed the first responders at the Templeton house to seize all cups and items that had been drunk or eaten prior to her collapse, an hour had passed. DI Christie decided to go and pay the Reverend a visit himself and get his version of events.

Reverend Brian Davenport was surprised at his late-night visit, but said it was understandable given the circumstances. Adam, who'd never warmed to the man, sarcastically thought that was very magnanimous of him.

'How is she?' He'd finally asked after showing the detective into his lounge.

'I don't know yet, we've not had a condition update. I'd like to know what happened, I understand you were with her at the time.'

'Yes indeed, it was really quite upsetting,' he replied sipping on what DI Christie suspected was a hot chocolate. He noticed that he wasn't offered one.

'We'd been talking, and I had said some prayers with her and she'd asked me about the fact that Jasper had never been baptised. I mean we don't ban people from the churchyard nowadays just because they've not been baptised, not like they used to in the old days. I was reassuring her about that when she came over faint and collapsed. Her sister was there in the room, she can tell you.'

'Had she been eating or drinking anything?'

'Just some tea. We all had tea.'

'You're not suggesting that somebody has purposely tried to hurt Margaret are you?'

'Without a clear understanding as to what has been happening, we have to keep an open mind.'

'Oh, I see. Well, that's very worrying.'

Adam had left the reverend to his "worries" and driven over to the hospital to see how Margaret was, and to speak to her sister. It had been a tiring journey, battling to retain his concentration in the heavy rain, and he'd been relieved when he'd finally pulled up in the hospital car park. Before he sought out Margaret and her sister, he grabbed himself a double expresso.

The bright white lights of the hospital corridors were an affront to his tired eyes, but he'd managed to track down Ciara O'Donoghue just as she was leaving the observation ward.

'She's stable. They don't think it was a heart attack, more likely a panic attack and just emotional exhaustion from the past week. They're going to keep her in for observation. That Reverend Davenport hadn't helped with all his fire and brimstone talk. I think he wound her up, he was certainly not comforting her.'

Adam heaved a sigh of relief that he wasn't going to have another Templeton death to deal with and after having a word with hospital security to ensure nobody without the right clearance, was allowed to see her, he'd driven Ciara back to the house.

'We've a new family liaison coming over, they'll stay with you tonight,' he'd told her.

'I don't need babysitting,' she'd replied defiantly.

'I know. But I will sleep better knowing that there's somebody here who can support you and Margaret when she comes out, if you need it.'

'You're not like the villagers, surely you don't believe in the Templeton curse?' She'd turned to him.

'No, I don't believe in ancient curses and vampires, but at present I have no logical explanation for the events of the past two weeks and so I'd like to err on the side of caution.'

'And what about your mysterious Dr Lane who came to visit? What does he think?'

'He's helping us with the investigation, but you must understand that he's only been here two days. We need to let him carry out his own enquiries and see where it leads us.'

As Adam Christie said that he'd silently wished to himself that Harrison Lane could somehow pull a miracle out of the hat for them very soon, and get to the bottom of their mystery. When he woke up in the morning to see the brief text from him saying he'd been called away on an urgent matter and so couldn't continue the investigation today, it had been a huge disappointment, to say the least. He hoped that the urgent matter would be over and done with ASAP.

26

'You're looking remarkably well for a dead man,' Harrison growled at Desmond Manning. He towered over him, at least twice his bulk. Everything about Harrison Lane was threatening, from his stance, and his expression, to his voice. Desmond Manning pressed himself against the wall of his hallway as hard as he could, but he couldn't escape the oppressive figure of the man in front of him.

'You're not going to hurt me,' his voice broke slightly with the fear that had tightened around his throat. 'You work for the police, your career would be over.'

'You forget, I can't hurt a dead man. You don't exist anymore. Nobody knows that you or I are here. Do they?'

That thought had clearly not registered in Desmond's brain until that moment, and Harrison saw him swallow hard.

'What do you want?' He'd rasped back.

'I want information and you're going to give it to me.'

Harrison had yanked the old man away from his defensive position on the wall and shoved him back through the doorway into the lounge area. The TV was still on, a muted chat show with a group of women laughing about something that neither Harrison nor Desmond would ever know. Harrison pushed Desmond into his armchair and pulled up a small stool that he clearly used to put his feet on, and sat down on it, facing the man who he'd been hunting for years.

'I didn't kill your mother,' was Desmond's opening gambit.

'Really! So you know she didn't kill herself. Why should I believe it wasn't you?'

'I swear. It wasn't.'

'So if it wasn't you, who was it?'

Desmond's thin dry lips opened and closed for a moment while he struggled with what to say next.

'I don't know,' was all he could manage.

'Oh, I think you can do a bit better than that. Do you really think I rode all this way to visit you, just to hear you don't know?'

The old man slowly shook his head.

'It wasn't us.'

'Why did my mother come back from America?'

Desmond's grey eyes searched Harrison's face.

'You really don't know anything do you?'

Harrison clenched his jaw.

'How about I start beating it out of you so that I can find out?'

The initial shock had started to leave Desmond's face and his eyes flickered over his captor's features, trying to work out how to worm his way out of the current situation.

'You're going to let me go then are you, if I tell you what you want?'

Harrison hadn't thought of the answer to that question.

'Yes. If you answer honestly.' He lied.

'And you think I believe you?'

'Perhaps I should just kill you now then? Let you go and join Freda?'

A ripple of hatred went across Desmond's face.

'If you kill me, then you'll never know who your father is. I know.' Desmond started.

'That your trump card?' Harrison spat back. 'Well, you're too late, I already know.'

Another look of shock travelled across Desmond's face, but he quickly recovered.

'So you know your mother wasn't the angel you thought she was then?' he quickly retorted.

That one hit home.

Harrison tried not to show any emotion, concentrating on keeping his face hard and unmoving, but Desmond must have seen something, because he pushed harder.

'You always blamed us for everything. She brought that man into the group and it was him, your father who killed Annette. Nearly got us all sent down. She was alright, did a runner with you to America. We had to stay behind and clean up.'

The realisation that his mother hadn't been escaping the Mannings, but his own father, knocked Harrison hard, but it made sense.

'So. Why did she come back? You must know that. Did you make her?'

Desmond shook his head. 'No.'

Harrison was getting impatient.

'I know it wasn't my dad who killed her, he was already in prison. After we'd returned, she came back to your group, and it was you who betrayed her, you who claimed she had hung herself. You murdered her.'

Harrison hadn't been aware of the fact he'd got up from the stool and was now leaning over Desmond in the chair, his hands balled into tight fists, ready to smash into his face.

He really wanted to smash that face with its bloodshot grey eyes that were too close together, and the white stubble covering a weak jawline and chin. The face on which a thin smile slowly formed as Desmond began a slow laugh.

'Ah like father, like son. That anger. I remember it well.'

Harrison took a few deep breaths and let his fists relax.

'Last chance Desmond. If I'm so like my father then you're about to face a painful death. Perhaps you're right because I know I'll enjoy it. I've waited long enough.'

Desmond was rigid in the chair, his eyes darting everywhere, trying to find a way out, unable to see anything but the big angry man in front of him. Eventually he shrugged.

'Means nothing to me. I'll tell you. Your mother was a dropout. Looking for a spiritual awakening, some kind of meaning to her life. We offered her freedom and something to believe in.'

'You offered her a twisted belief system that you used for your own ends. She'd seen you both as nurturing, caring figures who could help her, but you just used people.'

'We gave her a home. She was the one who brought that man and all the trouble into our lives.'

'You're not trying to play the victim on me again?'

'You think your father was the worst of it? Your mother came back because she had unfinished business. The goody two shoes gene you've obviously inherited. She came back to be a hero and bring down a man who makes your father look like a bloody angel.'

Desmond glared at Harrison. He felt his heart freeze.

'She was an informant, working with the police, only

naïve little Isabel didn't realise that the police weren't always the good guys. Someone betrayed her. So no, I don't know who actually killed her, and I wasn't about to try to find out. All I know is it was somebody with powerful connections.'

'She was working with the police? How? Doing what?'

'Gathering information is all I know. Funnily enough, she never told us any details.'

'Information on who?'

'Now that is where I stop. You see whatever you do to me, whether you kill me or torture me, it's almost certainly not going to be as bad as what he'll do to me if he finds out I told you anything. They never found the evidence she'd gathered. We thought she'd sent it to you somehow. That day she died, she was acting oddly, scared. She'd sent you away because she must have known something was going down and she wanted to protect her precious little boy. She disappeared out and then, when she came back it was like something had changed. A couple of hours later we found her dead. She brought a great shit storm down on us, it cost me to get the investigation buried.'

'You paid the police off?'

'Well, let's just say I did someone a favour. Had to give up a trump card I'd been holding for leverage to make sure we didn't get the blame. It took some interesting photographs of a senior officer that I'd acquired.'

'Did anyone find the evidence she'd gathered?'

'No. We had a nice return visit from your mother's friend, they trashed the place looking for it. We decided to move on, lie low. Freda never forgave your mother for ruining our lives like that. She'd loved that place. Look at this shit hole we ended up in. We lost everything.'

'I don't care about you. I want to know who it is. Who he is?'

Desmond shook his head.

'He was powerful then, now he's untouchable. Without evidence you've got no hope, but he'll have you and me killed all the same.'

Harrison stood up and paced in front of Desmond. Thinking.

In the background the sound of sirens nearby, broke into the tension of the room.

'How do I know you're telling me the truth?'

Desmond shrugged.

There was a banging on the front door. A fist on the wood which made them both jump. Then the sound of the door opening and shutting. Both men turned their heads in shock.

Harrison's heart began to thump hard in his chest. He looked at Desmond, but he was just as surprised as him. He wasn't expecting anyone. Who had the key? Who could just walk into Desmond's house?

Footsteps in the hallway.

A man.

Neither of them breathed.

Harrison prepared to fight, every muscle in his body coiled ready to launch at whoever it was that walked through that doorway.

Then the blond head of DS Jack Salter appeared around the corner. Harrison let out a breath of relief just as Jack's face also registered the same emotion at the sight of Desmond Manning still in one piece.

'Harrison,' he said nodding at him as though he'd just walked into a cafe and seen him at a table. 'Desmond Manning, I am arresting you on suspicion of the murder of Tyler Ford.'

As Jack read Desmond his rights and handcuffed his

wrists, Harrison saw two police cars screech to a halt in the street outside and officers poured out, some ran round the back while others approached the front door.

Everything was a blur for Harrison. His head felt light. He hadn't moved from the spot and he looked down to see his fists still curled ready to throw a punch.

His ears registered the hammering on the front door, Jack's voice reading Desmond his rights. Then...

'Harrison. Harrison!' Jack shouted. 'Open the front door, let them in.'

He looked at his friend as though he'd seen him for the first time.

'The front door. Let the tactical team in.'

He wasn't sure if his legs would work, but they did. He followed Jack's instruction and walked to the front door, opened it, raising his arms and pointed to the living room where Jack had finished reading Desmond his rights.

'Good timing,' he heard Jack say to them. 'DS Jack Salter, I called it in. That's my colleague Dr Harrison Lane in the hallway.'

'He broke into my house, he's been holding me prisoner, threatening me,' Desmond screeched at the tactical squad who had filled the lounge area. Spittle was coming out of his mouth in anger, his face red with the frustration. He pointed towards Harrison who'd come back into the room.

'Him. He held me hostage.'

Jack laughed.

'Nice try Mr Manning. You know that you let us in. I think your neighbours will be able to corroborate how I knocked on the front door and you opened it literally just a minute ago. Harrison came via the back to make sure you didn't escape. I've read him his rights. He's all yours.' Jack smiled at the officer in charge and stepped back to let them finish the arrest.

Harrison stared at the incandescent Desmond Manning who had now resorted to hurling every expletive ever invented, at anyone in the room. He looked like a skinny old man. Impotent and weak. His lounge was a dirty mess of furniture that had probably been dragged out of skips or off the dump, and the carpet was stained and worn threadbare. This was the sum total of the man Harrison had hated, even been afraid of, since he was a teenager.

Harrison walked out. He didn't even give Desmond Manning one last look. He walked out of the room, down the hallway and outside into the street, where he sat down on the doorstep. He didn't care about the little crowd of neighbours who had gathered in the street to see what all the fuss was about. He didn't care how cold it was, or feel the chill seep up from the concrete step. He just sat and let his blood pressure slowly return to normal, and the events of the last hour sink into his head. He had absolutely no idea of how Jack was here, or the other police officers, other than Ryan must have been behind it. All he cared about was the information he'd just managed to get out of Desmond Manning.

AT SOME POINT, he wasn't sure how much time had gone by, Jack put his hand on Harrison's shoulder and told him it was time to leave.

He got up and followed him, like an automaton, down the front path and to Jack's car.

'My bike!' He said to Jack.

'You're in no state to ride. Get in the car and we'll go somewhere, get something to eat and drink. Talk. Then I'll bring you back. It will be fine where it is, there's going to be so many police going in and out, nobody's going to nick it.'

Harrison did as he was told again, climbing into the passenger seat.

'We need to call Ryan, let him know you're OK. He'll be going spare.'

Harrison didn't reply, so Jack pulled his phone out and started to dial.

'Did you get what you needed from Manning?' He asked.

Harrison gave a tiny nod. 'Most of it.'

'Ryan, it's Jack. It worked, well done mate. Went smoothly. He's OK but I think he's in a bit of shock. I'm taking him somewhere to get something to eat and then we'll call you later. Yeah, arrested and all above board without a mark on him.'

Harrison stared out of the passenger side window at a woman in a flowing flowery dress with blonde hair. She smiled at him and waved.

27

It took about half an hour after they'd driven away from the Manning property, before Harrison started to feel the shakes. As his adrenaline levels plummeted it left him drained and exhausted. Jack made him drink a hot chocolate and eat an omelette, neither of which he'd really wanted, but he knew that the sugar would help give his brain a boost of energy to recover, while the protein in the eggs would help his body. After an hour of feeling shaky, he finally started to feel like he was returning to normal.

For most of that time, neither of them said anything. Jack let him just sit there, staring into the distance, just processing the last few hours. He knew Harrison's brain needed time to catch up, it was in emergency recovery mode, looking after the vital organs after having pumped all of its energies and focus into his muscles for what it believed to be a fight for survival. He'd seen it and he'd experienced it himself.

Finally, Harrison looked up at him and spoke.

'So where the hell did you appear from?'

Jack gave him a huge grin.

'Welcome back Doc. You've got your assistant to thank for the masterful plan.'

Harrison leaned back in the cafe chair and listened.

'Once Ryan had tracked Desmond down, he knew you'd want some time with him, but he was also worried you might overstep the mark and not end up arresting him, or getting yourself into trouble. Particularly relevant bearing in mind Gordon Jacobsen has already got his eye on you. Well, clearly Ryan loves his job and doesn't want his boss to be arrested for perverting the course of justice. So, he timed it all perfectly. He gave you an hour's head start. Enough time to gain entry and start interrogating the little scrote. Have to say he had a lot of faith in you to not just beat the shit out of him, because that's what I thought you were going to do. Anyway, he had a stroke of genius. Realised that the house Desmond had holed up in was where he'd been living with Freda. He remembered that Freda had a set of keys in the handbag found at the fire, which was being held as evidence. He was able to get a copy of that key - an act which I don't want to know anything about for obvious reasons as a serving officer - and he gave it to me. Unfortunately, I seem to have now mislaid it.' Jack smiled one of his cheeky grins. 'Anyway, I was to wait outside until I heard police sirens approaching, or unless I thought you were in any trouble - or causing it. He had tipped Gordon Jacobsen off, saying the intel was from us. Once the sirens were close, I was to bang on the front door and ask to come in, and make a lot of noise so that the neighbours would see. I had to open the door with the key and pretend that Desmond had opened it for me. That way we gained lawful entry and were able to make the arrest all above board and I could plan any excuses if I found that Desmond had a broken nose - or worse. If you had smashed anything trying to get in, then I was just going to say you heard a scuffle and thought I was in trouble, so had to force entry rather than wait for me to let you in. I did check before we left and couldn't see any issues, so I assume you got in through a window, or forced your way in the front door?'

'Bedroom window.'

'Good. So, what do you think? Pretty clever plan of the crisp munching geek don't you think?'

Jack beamed at Harrison.

Harrison had to admit he was impressed by the plan, even if he'd been somewhat kept in the dark by his assistant.

'The question is,' continued Jack, 'Did Manning give you the information you wanted?'

Harrison let out a big sigh and looked out through the cafe window. Voicing it out loud would make it that much more real, but the story had to be told.

'Yeah, he answered most of my questions, at least, those which served him. He admitted that my mother was murdered, but said it wasn't them. He claimed she'd been a police informant, gathering evidence against someone who was powerful who she had unfinished business with.'

'Did you believe him?'

Harrison thought for a moment. 'Yeah, yeah I did. What he said fits with the woman I remember, and although he wouldn't have wanted to admit it if he'd been the killer, I don't think it was him somehow.'

'So what happened?'

'Someone betrayed her.'

'Who?'

'Who betrayed her? No idea. I don't think Desmond knew either, but he reckons it was someone inside the Force.'

'Who's the man she was gathering evidence on?'

'That he wouldn't tell me. Said if he found out then he'd have a slow and painful death.'

'Did he say anything about your father? Genetic father?' Jack asked more gently.

'Said he killed Annette for sure. Sounds like my mother fell in love with him, and he manipulated her. She had to leave with me for the States to get away from him after Nunhead. I know she always saw the best in people. Some would call it naivety, but I think it was just her good heart.'

'So she came back when he went to jail?'

'That might have been one reason, but she also came back to settle her score with the mystery man. I just don't know what he'd done to make her so determined to get him, and I don't know who he is.'

Jack slumped back in his chair and looked at his friend.

'Can't believe you resisted even taking one swing at him,' he smiled.

'I came close, but I figured that if I did let rip, I'd probably break his jaw and he wouldn't have been able to talk.'

Jack smirked and then his face became serious.

'At least you know Manning is now going to spend the rest of his years in prison. And most importantly you have some answers. You know you were right that your mother was killed, she didn't take her own life. More than that, your mother died because she was trying to do something good.'

'Yeah, yeah I do and that means a lot. I'd questioned everything over the last few days. Started to think that maybe I'd corrupted my memories to create a more wholesome view of her than was true, but I hadn't. She was everything I thought she was and more. I know she fell for a psychopath, but that's their talent right? Manipulation, lying, charm. I know that, I've met enough of them over the years. I don't know when he started killing, maybe Annette was the first, or maybe she was just one in a long line even before he started on the murders he got convicted for. But he's where he should be.'

'Absolutely.'

'I also know that I'm not like him. I've inherited my mother's traits, her sense of right, and her compassion. I suspect she was going after the mystery man because of what he'd done to people she loved and knew. She always fought for the victims and the weak. That's always been her legacy and I'm going to continue to live by it.'

Jack had nothing to say to that, he just smiled at the big man in front of him who he'd never known let anyone down on that promise. It was good to have him back.

28

Harrison stayed with Jack until after lunch. With the initial shock and stress over and done with, the pair of them rediscovered their appetites and had tucked into a decent lunch.

'I'm going to miss working with you,' Jack said. 'Now you're high and mighty in the NCA, you won't want to get your hands dirty with any of our weird crimes in the Met.'

'If you get any weird crimes, as you so incorrectly call them, you know I'll be on the case. I'll be covering the whole of the UK so that still includes London.'

'Well, don't forget us, I'll treat you to a Diet Coke and steak pie and chips if you help us out.'

'How could I possibly forget you Jack,' Harrison smiled back.

'And make sure I get a wedding invite, I like a good party,' Jack winked at him.

Harrison raised his eyebrows and felt a flutter at the thought, but he wasn't sure if it was panic or excitement.

Jack took him back to the Manning's road and his bike. As

they drove past, they saw a forensic team were on site. One of them was just walking out the house with white coveralls on, and see through evidence bags, filled with something, in their hands. Harrison wondered what else might come to light in the detritus of the Manning household.

He'd contemplated spending a night somewhere local, and riding back in the morning, worried that he might be too tired to do the journey, but in the end he got a second wind. It was just as Joe had said, the minute he found himself and his purpose again, he felt rejuvenated; and the most important thing was to get to the bottom of the deaths in Yorkshire and make sure that nobody else was going to suffer.

DI ADAM CHRISTIE WAS SURPRISED, but delighted when he saw Harrison walk into his incident room later that afternoon.

'Glad to see you're back,' he beamed, 'I hope you managed to sort out the emergency.'

'I did. It was something that had been niggling at the back of my mind for some time, so I'm here with a clear head to crack on.'

Adam Christie heaved an internal sigh of relief.

'Margaret Templeton collapsed last night. Suspected heart attack, but she was fine, just a panic attack and exhaustion. They've kept her in for observations and put her on a drip and eating plan. I don't think she's been looking after herself the last few days. Her sister went home to find the dog had been sick and what it had eaten looked remarkably like the dinner she'd fed to Margaret earlier, so she thinks she was probably not eating her own food and giving it to the dog to get her sister off her back. Not really surprising, poor woman.'

'She's lost all those she loved, it must be hard to keep going,' Harrison said.

'Indeed. Our friendly fire and brimstone vicar had been there when she collapsed, so I seized all the cups and tea for testing, just in case. They came back all clear, but I don't think Ciara O'Donoghue is going to let him cross the threshold again. He doesn't exactly have a comforting bedside manner.'

Harrison thought Adam Christie was probably understating it, but the vicar didn't matter. The most important thing now was to help Margaret and find the answers as to why she'd lost her family. He walked straight over to the desk he'd been using and logged into the system.

Harrison decided to take a piece of his own advice, follow what he'd said when he'd first arrived on the case and treat each death individually. Perhaps they were trying to force a series of random instances into one neat motive and that was why they weren't getting anywhere. Richard Templeton was the first to die. He had no history of heart problems and had even got that medically confirmed not long before his death. His heart attack was therefore surprising based on his fitness levels. That was where Harrison would start.

Harrison worked through the timeframes again based on all the witness statements. His argument with Bob and the reverend, his discussion about selling the house with John Rowland, and then the decision to go to the blood stone and see what was buried underneath it. Nobody would ever know Richard's true motivations for going to the stone that day. Was it to find treasure, or was it to dispel a legend that was about to be capitalised on by those other than his own family? It was believed he went alone to the stone, but that couldn't be proven. It was also believed that all he found were a few old spear and arrowheads, but again, that couldn't be proven. All Harrison could do was work with the evidence and the facts he had.

He moved from the statements to the autopsy report. Instead of looking for similarities to the other deaths, he just focused on this being one isolated case. Was there anything unusual which might have been missed? Autopsies follow standard procedures, there were a set of general tests which were conducted, and then if there was a particular suspicion, then that might involve other more specialised tests. He could see that in Richard's case, it had just been the standard procedure, which, on the face of it, was quite understandable. There'd been nothing to suggest a suspicious death other than the victim's own fitness levels and some ancient stories.

'I'd like to go and take a look at Richard Templeton and speak to the pathologist.' Harrison appeared at DI Christie's desk, making him jump.

'No problem. Scott, can you arrange that for Dr Lane?'

Scott Haynes' body language was reminiscent of a stroppy teenager asked to do the washing up. Harrison wasn't taking anymore crap from the man. He didn't care what he thought of him, this wasn't about either of them, it was about Richard Templeton and his family.

'I need to see them today,' Harrison said firmly.

Haynes gritted his teeth and threw a contemptuous look at both Harrison and his boss.

'It's already four o'clock,' he whined.

'Plenty of time then,' Adam Christie replied, clearly irritated by his attitude - almost as much as Harrison. 'Sort it please.'

Haynes got on the phone, roughly punching the numbers into the handset and turning his back on Harrison.

'Dr Niven, DS Scott Haynes. I'm so sorry to bother you at this time of day, but we have a visiting psychologist who has asked if he could see Richard Templeton's remains and have a word with you.'

There was a pause as he listened.

'Are you sure we're not imposing, I appreciate it's nearly home time?' The DS was clearly disappointed that the pathologist was being so accommodating. 'OK, thank you. We'll see you in half an hour then.' He virtually threw the handset back down and turned to face DI Christie, ignoring Harrison. 'Dr Niven has been helpful and said we can go now, it will take us half an hour to get there. Do you need me to come back in after?' He added, hopefully.

'Yeah please. Bring Dr Lane back and make sure there's nothing else that needs doing today would you?' That was an order rather than a question and Haynes knew it.

'Right, let's go,' he said curtly to Harrison, and walked out of the office.

'Don't leave him in the mortuary will you!' Adam Christie said laughing to Harrison as he followed in his wake. 'They will count the bodies you know.'

Harrison smirked back. 'The thought had never crossed my mind,' he replied with fake innocence.

'ARE you trained in pathology as well as psychology?' Haynes sarcastically asked Harrison in the car.

Harrison knew they had a half hour journey and he could see just how Haynes and his bad mood, were going to spend it.

'Did you know that you can taste what people are

thinking, even if they've died?'

'Taste? What do you mean?' Haynes looked horrified, attempting to look at Harrison and still keep his eyes on the road.

'It's the latest research. Goes back to when we were animals. When someone is frightened, it shows itself in the chemicals in our bodies, just by licking the skin of the deceased can help you to determine their mood just prior to death.'

'What the?... you must be kidding. You're going to go to the mortuary and lick a cadaver?' Hayne's mouth was open. 'That's sick.'

'Yeah.'

'Yeah what?' Hayne's voice had risen a couple of octaves.

'Yeah, I'm joking,' Harrison replied and turned to look out of the side window so that the DS couldn't see the huge smirk on his face.

'For fuck's sake,' Haynes replied, muttering a few more expletives about Harrison to himself.

It did the trick. It shut him up for the rest of the journey.

At the mortuary, Haynes informed him that he was going to go and get a coffee while Harrison went in.

'Dr Niven's office is through there,' he gesticulated dismissively. 'I'll be in the cafe.'

Harrison suspected that the detective thought he was being rude and annoying him by walking off, but he more than did him a favour. After the day he'd already had, his patience was wearing thin and DI Christie's suggestion had become more than appealing.

Dr Rachel Niven turned out to be a charming woman in her late fifties with a calming manner and soothing voice. She was just what he needed and was more than happy to help him.

'I have to say I was surprised that his heart had arrested, it looked in top shape for someone of his age and there were no issues with blood vessels, valves, clots. All clear.'

She showed Harrison into an autopsy suite where the cadaver of the late Richard Templeton was laid out on a metal inspection gurney. It felt colder in the room than it did outside and Harrison wondered how many layers the staff had to wear to keep warm. Richard had obviously already undergone an autopsy and so his body had been opened up and his internal organs taken out for inspection. It was never a pleasant sight seeing another human like this, bloodless and eviscerated, but Harrison took comfort in knowing it was always done with care and with their best interests at heart. Discovering the cause of death was the first step to getting justice for a victim.

'I understand it was just the standard tests done?' Harrison asked.

'Yes, that's what budgets allow for. We'll only undertake more extensive laboratory testing if it's specifically requested. I have to say though, that there was no indication of a chemical interference.'

'What about natural?'

'What do you mean?'

'It's often easier to spot the man-made chemicals, but what if some kind of poison had been administered that occurs naturally?'

'Like a plant-based substance?' Dr Niven thought carefully. 'That's of course absolutely possible and sometimes harder to pick up. There weren't any indications of irritation in his throat or oesophagus, or in his intestines however. His tongue was normal size. That might indicate it wasn't ingested orally, if a poison was used.'

They were standing over Richard's remains. It was never

Harrison's favourite task in murder enquiries, but it often helped him to get a clearer picture of the victim's last unfortunate moments which couldn't always be gleaned from the words and photographs of the autopsy report.

'No signs of needle entry?'

'I haven't found one, but if you think we could be looking at something like that, then I'm happy to take another look over him to be absolutely sure.'

'Thank you, and the grazes on the knee?'

'When he fell as he died. There's also a cut on his arm. No bruising so we know he died instantly.'

Harrison nodded. His eyes scanning every inch of the unfortunate man who lay in front of him. Even in death, he had a kind face and as Dr Niven had said; he looked fit. There was no middle-aged spread, his arms and legs were sinewy, not bulked, but muscular.

'He has a couple of blisters on his hands,' Dr Niven said, turning the palms towards Harrison. 'They weren't fresh from that day, I'd say probably a couple of days old, but he had broken them open again during his digging. You'd have thought he'd at least have worn plasters or gloves to protect his hands.'

'His wife said he'd been digging a drainage ditch that week. Hard work, even for someone like him, so perhaps that's where he'd got them.'

'That would make sense, they look to be in the kind of place you'd find them if you were grasping a shovel handle.'

That helped Harrison understand Richard's state of mind better. If you were planning to go and dig something up, and you already had blisters on your hands, you'd think about protecting them. The fact he didn't, meant he was focused on the task. There was an urgency or obsessiveness there. The dead could always find a way to tell you things.

. . .

Harrison left Dr Niven and her assistant giving Richard another once over for needle marks. He was relieved to leave the smell of death and the chemicals needed to preserve it, and swap them for the aroma of coffee. DS Haynes was sitting reading a discarded copy of The Sun, his coffee cup empty apart from a foamy brown residue.

'You done? Find anything?'

'It was useful, yes.' Harrison replied.

Haynes got up and flung the newspaper back down on the table beside him. 'I can't stand them places, the smell of the dead soaks in through your pores.' He curled his nose up. 'Let's go then, it's already gone five.'

Just as they pulled into the incident room car park, Harrison's mobile rang.

'Dr Lane,' Harrison recognised the soothing tone of the pathologist, 'we've been over Richard again with a fine-tooth comb. My assistant, who has even better eyesight than me, has also been over him. We can't find any needle entry points.'

'Thank you Dr Niven, that's helpful.'

'My pleasure,' she'd said. Her helpful attitude contrasting the slam of the door as a stroppy DS Haynes got out the car.

Harrison didn't even notice. The jigsaw puzzle of Richard Templeton's death had started to take a shape. There was something that Haynes had said which sparked a memory, and that combined with what he'd seen at the mortuary had given him a very logical potential explanation. He just had to find the evidence to prove it.

29

Reception was closed, but the rest of the team were still in the incident room.

'How did it go?' Christie asked Harrison as he walked back in. Harrison could see the look of hope and anticipation on his face.

'I need the report on the spear and arrowheads,' he said, not wasting time with social chat.

'Right. Scott? Where can Dr Lane find that?'

DS Haynes had been in the process of shutting down his computer for the day.

'Report?'

'You said they'd been analysed,' Harrison replied. 'I need to see what was tested and the results.' He was losing patience with the man, fast.

'Well, Yeah, they were looked at, but we didn't think there was any need to do any specific tests as such. I told you they're nothing more than some old bits of tribal stuff. If you want to see them for yourself they're in the evidence room.'

Christie saw the look on Harrison's face and moved quickly to disperse the storm that was about to hit his DS.

'There's a bit of a backlog down there, Chris Taylor was taken ill. So why don't you help Dr Lane out and get them ordered for him?' He said through gritted teeth, even he was getting to the end of his patience with Haynes and was contemplating allowing Harrison to tear a strip off him.

'I'm bloody starving, not had a break,' Haynes moaned, oblivious to the effect he was having on both men. He looked at his boss, gave a big sigh and stomped out the room, but not before he'd given Harrison another one of his filthy looks. The other three members of the team all exchanged raised eyebrow glances.

Harrison went straight to his computer and did some research. The British Museum site held some of the information he was looking for, and there had been another article he'd read some time ago which had given him an idea.

Twenty minutes later, he was losing patience.

'Should I go to the evidence room now?' He asked Adam.

'Give him another couple of minutes, he'll get it sorted.'

Harrison couldn't sit still any longer, so he walked to the water refill station in the corridor to fill up his bottle and to stop himself from pacing up and down the office. When he returned, Haynes was at his desk, laughing and joking with something in his hand which he chucked onto the desk when he saw Harrison.

'Got your cursed tribal tat for you Dr Lane,' he sneered.

Harrison strode over. 'You've taken them out the evidence bag?'

'Yeah, it's not like they're a murder weapon is it?' Haynes replied dismissively and unwrapped a pre-packaged sandwich, which had no doubt been one of the reasons why he'd taken so long to return.

On Harrison's desk was an old dirty, leather cloth, lying on top of an evidence bag, and on top of that was an old spear head, and two arrowheads with broken shafts.

'You were playing with these!' Harrison suddenly said to DS Haynes, causing everyone in the room to stop what they were doing and look up at the force of his question.

Haynes's face changed, he wasn't sure whether to be angry or scared at the tone of the big man in front of him.

'I was just having a laugh, what's wrong with you? They're not...' But the last words disappeared in shock.

Harrison had leapt across the room, his right arm flying straight at him and striking his sandwich out of his grasp. It flew across the room, slamming into the floor with a splat. Then he'd grabbed both of Haynes's wrists yanking them, palm upwards, and looked at them.

'What the hell are you doing?' Haynes squeaked. 'This is assault.'

'Dr Lane?' Adam Christie shouted. He and Sergeant Cutter had both stood up and were weighing up their chances of being able to tackle Harrison before he slaughtered the DS. Lucy was sat at her desk in shock and Andy Nesbitt, had his hand on the phone ready to call for back-up.

'I'm potentially saving your life,' Harrison growled back at him. After inspecting his hands, he roughly let them go, flinging them to his sides, before stepping back away from him. He turned to DI Christie.

'I think Richard Templeton was killed by those bits of tribal tat as DS Haynes called them.' He turned back to Haynes, 'I suggest you go and give your hands a really good wash. You're lucky you don't have any cuts on them or right now we'd be trying to resuscitate you.'

Haynes stood open-mouthed looking at his hands. 'What? How?'

'Can you explain Dr Lane?' Adam asked.

'I believe they're coated in poison,' Harrison looked straight at the DI and the conviction on his face persuaded him.

'Someone go with Scott, so he doesn't touch any door handles. Get your hands washed thoroughly. I'll call a team in to take these arrowheads in for testing.' DI Christie instantly took charge.

'The man in the evidence room, you said he was taken ill?' Harrison questioned.

It took a moment for the penny to drop.

'Bloody hell, yes, heart again. He's OK, they got to him quickly when he started feeling ill.' Christie said. 'We never connected it. How sure are you that they're poisoned?'

'Dr Niven said she was surprised by the fact Richard died of a heart attack, there was nothing to indicate that he was at risk. So, if it was highly unlikely that he'd died naturally, that meant something had poisoned him. I worked through the various methods someone might have administered poison to induce a heart seizure. The fact of where he was, and that there was no food or drink with him, ruled out a lot of methods. There were also no indications he'd ingested poison, and no needle marks if it had been injected. What he did have were open blisters on his palms. We knew that Henry Templeton had been to Malaysia. It was common practice for arrow and spear heads to be coated in poison, the Upas tree is a well known and highly toxic source of poisonous latex that was used around south east Asia well into the 1800s. The poison acts fast, paralysing the nervous system and inducing cardiac arrest. There are examples like these in the British Museum, and the poison is just as deadly now as when it was first put on the arrows. If Haynes had a cut on his hand, or perhaps if he'd eaten some poison with his sandwich and it had got into his bloodstream, he'd be having a heart attack by now. Richard Templeton handled the arrow heads when he'd dug them up, the poison would have got into his bloodstream through the open blisters on his hands. I believe that if you get those arrow and spear heads properly analysed, then you'll find that they're coated in the cardiac glycoside antiarin, a lethal poison.'

DI Christie slumped back down into his chair.

'So Henry did bring a curse back with him. Why didn't he die then?'

'He was probably just lucky. Didn't have any open wounds and maybe didn't even take them out of the leather cloth. He may well have buried some other pieces of tribal art with them but they've rotted over the years without the protection of the leather. I would hazard a guess that these were once part of the stolen offerings to whatever god the temple they visited had been dedicated to. It would have been common practice for the tribes to ask for divine luck in their hunting.'

'And poor Richard ended up another victim. But what about Jasper and Lee? Neither of them could have touched these. They were in our custody by the time Jasper arrived and Lee died at his parents' home.'

'When I arrived, I said that the deaths may not be connected and maybe we were looking for a pattern where there wasn't one. We were searching for a motive that could account for all the deaths. Perhaps there isn't one. Perhaps each death is separate.'

DS Haynes had re-entered the room. He looked pale and decidedly sheepish. Harrison turned to him.

'Had these been thoroughly analysed when they came in, as you said they were, then you might have spared your colleague in the evidence room from almost losing his life and then nearly dying yourself. Everything has to be looked at and considered, nothing should be dismissed.'

Haynes looked at him and his boss, and for once, didn't say a word.

30

Charlotte wasn't sure how long she'd fainted for. She wasn't the world's best at keeping an eye on the time, as her mother always reminded her. She knew it was at least ten or fifteen minutes because she'd come back from school and run up the stairs to go to the toilet. The most mortifying part was that she'd wet herself on the toilet floor as she'd passed out.

She'd woken up, her hands and feet tingling and her head throbbing where she'd landed on the floor. She was so embarrassed, and grateful her parents weren't home to witness it, but it had been another warning.

Despite still feeling lightheaded, she set about clearing up her mess, putting her school uniform in the washing machine and mopping the toilet floor. By the time she'd finished, she was exhausted and lay down on her bed.

Staring up at the ceiling, the morbid thoughts came back down, spiralling into her head. It was the curse, and it had nearly taken her. Would her parents come home from work and find her dead? Or would it take her in the night while they slept?

Charlotte opened her bedside drawer and took out the bible she had found on her parents' bookshelves, and she began to read it. If she prayed perhaps God would hear her, she could beat the evil with his help. Sometimes she believed that would work, other times, she knew that the blood which ran in her veins was tainted. It was that which had brought the curse on her and whatever she did; it was coming. There would be no stopping it, and it would be soon.

31

The adrenaline spike from Haynes's near death experience had given Harrison another resulting plummet in energy, and once he'd made sure the necessary tests were underway on the arrowheads, he decided to call it a day. It had been a long one.

'I thought you'd finally had enough of his whingeing,' Adam Christie had said to him, laughing, after Haynes had been sent to the medical bay for a second and more thorough cleaning of his hands.

'Have to say that was one great swat of the sandwich,' Sergeant Cutter smirked. 'Flew like a torpedo'. They all looked to where the sandwich, which had turned out to be a BLT on granary, had ended up. A damp patch remained in memory of the smeared tomato and mayonnaise which had oozed out of it on landing.

'It was the look on his face that got me.' Lucy giggled.

'Have to say I wasn't relishing the idea of trying to tackle you off him,' Adam added. 'I think we'd have had to taser you.'

'Thanks, that's good to know,' Harrison joined the joke. 'I'll watch out for that next time.'

It was welcome light relief for all the team after the disappointment and stress of the last few days. What was even better news was when the DI's phone rang just before Harrison left.

'Preliminary results,' he said to the team, covering the mouthpiece. 'Confirmed presence of antiarine.'

Sergeant Cutter gave a fist pump in celebration. He'd contemplated giving Harrison a high five, but thought better of it.

'Well done Harrison,' Adam said once he was off the phone. 'That's one down. We'll get Richard's remains tested again in the morning and I've no doubt we'll get a match. A tragic accident, but at least we can give Margaret some closure.'

Finding answers and getting closure were the themes of Harrison's day. He left the incident room for the pub with the knowledge that he'd at least made a start on them, both personally and professionally.

Harrison enjoyed the walk from the incident room to the pub. The rain had finally stopped and a thin mist hung in the cold December air. There was no doubt it was a picturesque village. Stone cottages and traditional shop fronts ran all the way along the main road, with little cobbled streets leading off to all sorts of oldy worldy Englishness: a quaint delicatessen shop, the Emporium of Curios and Antiques, or the village tea room. There was a strong sense of identity here, a close-knit community. It was no wonder that there was a feeling of shock, with such a small community losing so many people in such a short space of time.

At night it became a black and grey world and took on

an almost eerie feel, only countered by the cheery Christmas decorations which sprung out of every window or were hung from the traditional Victorian lampposts. They reminded Harrison that the festive season was nearly upon them. At the end of the high street, beyond the Druids Arms, the stone tower of the church rose up black and solid even against the night sky. He wondered how Reverend Davenport and Bob would take the news about Richard, but then reminded himself that there were still three more deaths to explain any one, or more, of which could yet be murder. Tomorrow he would focus on Jasper and Lee. Both young and both related, but were their deaths coincidences? Or were other forces at play?

Harrison went down to the bar for a quick meal, deciding to try Sally's steak pie and chips. It reminded him of his last evening in London and as soon as he'd finished, he went straight up to his room and rang Tanya, dialling her on the WhatsApp video call so he could see her. She was at home, curled on her sofa in the pink fleece she loved to wear when lounging in her flat. Harrison could see she'd been reading a book, and she looked sleepy herself, but listened intently as he'd recounted his meeting with Desmond Manning.

'You should be proud of yourself,' she'd said to him when he'd finished. 'I don't think many people would have been able to resist the urge to just thump him. The good news is that he's going to face justice which should mean he'll spend the rest of his life in jail. You've achieved what you set out to do.'

'Sort of,' Harrison had replied quietly. He'd not yet wanted to admit it, but while ensuring Desmond never walked the streets a free man again, had been satisfying, the conversation had opened up a whole new can of rotting worms. 'I still haven't found the person responsible for my mother's murder.'

Tanya looked sad at his words. 'But you have confirmed it wasn't suicide, you've given your mother back the truth.'

She was right, but was it enough?

They'd talked for another few minutes, with Tanya chatting about her day. She'd taken the day off work, left her forensic suit at home and instead gone Christmas shopping.

'I got my mother the perfect belt, dad's more awkward, I've ordered something for him online. Managed to find a brilliant present for the Secret Santa at work. I'll show you when you get back.'

He longed to be on the sofa next to her, his hand stroking her soft auburn hair, her head resting on his chest. Listening to her chat until he stopped the words from coming out of her mouth with a kiss. Could he make her happy? The contentment he'd found in her company had surprised him, it was as though he'd been wandering all his life and finally found a place where he wanted to stay, where he felt relaxed and safe. Was this love?

Eventually, Tanya said she should leave him to sleep. She'd never seen Harrison look so tired before, and he still had to get up tomorrow and finish the investigation. They'd exchanged good nights, and he'd gone straight to bed. His last thought before sleep overwhelmed him was the realisation he was going to have to get Tanya a Christmas present.

HARRISON'S first task in the morning, was to partake in another one of Sally's full English breakfasts. He'd had his best sleep in ages and the early night meant he'd slept a good nine hours. His brain felt rejuvenated, which was more than he could say for his body which hadn't taken too kindly to the long hours travelling on his bike, and the extreme stress which had kept his muscles tense for most of the day.

Penny seemed to have forgotten her wariness after his tourism question the first morning, and was chatting cheerfully to a couple who were eating their breakfast. When she saw Harrison walk in, she stopped and met him halfway across the bar.

'Reporter and photographer from the Daily Mail,' she said quietly and gave a slight tip of her head towards the couple. Then, 'Another full English for you Dr Lane?' This time her voice had returned to full cheery volume.

Harrison was grateful for the warning.

He parked himself on the table she'd prepared.

'Morning,' the woman said to him.

'Morning,' he'd replied politely.

He could tell they were scoping him out, trying to see if he was from a rival news agency or could in any way be useful to their story.

'What brings you here?' She asked nonchalantly, spiking a mushroom with her fork.

'Just visiting an old patient,' Harrison replied. He'd play on his title and let them think he was a GP or some other kind of doctor.

'Margaret Templeton?' She tried, shovelling in a large mouthful of sausage and egg.

'Who? No.' Harrison smiled back.

'Have you heard about the vampires that killed a woman, or the Templeton family curse?' She wasn't about to give up. 'Been in all the papers, everyone's talking about it.'

'I don't tend to read newspapers I'm afraid, too busy and they're usually just full of gossip. I prefer more academic reading,' he'd replied, purposely trying to snub her. She was a reporter and had a thick skin so his comment barely got a twitch of an eyebrow. He tried a different tactic and picked his phone out of his pocket, making a point of looking at it in the hope it would give her the message that he didn't want to talk to her.

'Here you are Dr Lane, your full English,' Penny placed the large plate of food in front of him.

'Beth and David are from the Daily Mail, they're going to run a story on the various legends in the village. Did you know we had a ghost at the pub?'

'I had heard,' Harrison replied.

'Said to be a heartbroken lover of Henry Templeton. There were quite of few of them in the village,' she winked at the reporter.

Harrison realised that this was a great opportunity for Penny and Sally's business, being mentioned in the Daily Mail could bring in a big surge of customers to their bed-and-breakfast business, and the pub. It made him all the more grateful that she'd warned him when he first came down and was keeping his real identity and links with the police, quiet. It was good to know she could be trusted.

The breakfast, although delicious, weighed him down for his walk back to the incident room, but it had been worth it; he probably wouldn't eat again until dinner.

He was early, the rest of the team hadn't yet arrived, and so he settled himself at his freshly cleaned desk, pulled all the reports and statements relating to Jasper and re-read every one.

There was no way that Jasper could have come into contact with the poisoned arrowheads, they were safely in police custody by the time he arrived at his parents' home to comfort his mother. He'd have liked to talk to Margaret again, see if she could give him any more information as to Jasper's state of mind on the night he died, but she was too ill. The hospital had kept her in. She seemed to have lost her will to live.

There was one person who hadn't given a statement, and that was Jasper's wife Shannon, who was still at their home with their baby son and apparently too frightened to visit for fear he might suffer the same fate as his father. As they lived a couple of hundred miles away, it wouldn't be easy for Harrison to go and interview her in person. In cases like this he would always choose to meet people in order to be able to study the interviewee's body language first hand, subtleties that didn't get carried in the voice. Instead, he arranged the next best thing, a video call with her for mid morning.

The rest of the team filtered in, minus DS Haynes.

'I've given him the day off,' Adam Christie told Harrison. 'He was in a bit of shock after sandwich-gate yesterday. His innate grumpiness was battling with recognising that he needed to apologise to you and be grateful that you saved his life. I'll let him wrestle with that one at home for another twenty-four hours.'

Harrison thought back to the satisfaction he'd got from whacking the sandwich out of Haynes's hand and was more than relieved he didn't have to put up with his annoying interference today, even if he would have enjoyed watching him eat humble pie.

'There's a Daily Mail reporter and photographer staying at the pub, no doubt they'll be sniffing around.'

The DI sighed. 'Yup, already had at least ten missed calls. They clocked your involvement?'

'No. Penny was discreet, warned me.'

'Good lass. I've no doubt she'll want the publicity for the

pub, but we close ranks around here and she'll not want anything stopping the investigation. We'll be holding a press conference later, release the information about Richard, once I've let Margaret know. That'll give them something to get their fangs into today. It's not as juicy as a family curse, but poisoned arrowheads are sexier than a simple middle-aged heart attack. You need anything from us?'

'I'm on it. Speaking to Shannon Templeton in about an hour, then I'm going to go round to Lizzie Meyer, Lee Rowland's girlfriend. Neither of them have been spoken to because they weren't in the vicinity of the deceased at the time.'

'Do you want me to sit in on the interviews?'

'No, you're good. I just need to crack on.'

'OK. I was going to take a couple of hours off this afternoon, need to get the wife's Christmas present or I'm going to end up as the turkey. You've got my mobile, if you need anything just call.'

DI Christie recognised the change in Harrison from the first couple of days that he'd been with them. He was focused and determined. He now had real hope that they could finally dispel the crazy curse and vampire theories sooner rather than later. He was tired of fighting off the media and trying to defend an investigation that was all smoke and mirrors. At least they had firm evidence for one death. Just three to go. In the meantime, he had a critical quest to undertake. He'd already tried two shops, and they'd been sold out. Failure was not an option. His Christmas Day depended on it.

32

Shannon Templeton turned out to be a redhead with a core of motherly steel.

'I'm not worried about myself,' she told Harrison within seconds of their call starting, 'but I'm not risking Zack by bringing him anywhere near that village.'

Harrison didn't want to point out that if the curse was real, then distance wasn't the issue, it would go on bloodline wherever they lived. He didn't of course, apart from the fact it wasn't true anyway, she was clearly already distraught after losing her husband. Behind her, Harrison could see a little blonde boy in a playpen, happily chewing on some kind of brightly coloured soft toy and gurgling away to himself.

He knew that Adam Christie had gone to the hospital, en route to his Christmas shopping, and informed Margaret about the cause of Richard's death. He'd asked Harrison to tell Shannon before it was broadcast in the media. The family should know first.

'I wanted to let you know about Richard, Jasper's father. We've discovered that the cause of his death was accidental poisoning. The tribal arrowheads and spearheads that he'd dug up the day he died, were coated in poison. It's something that was quite commonly used by Malaysian hunters, and many others. A natural poison that resulted in the victim suffering a coronary arrest.'

'Poison? You're kidding. That was like a hundred and fifty years ago or something.'

'Yes. It can survive for hundreds, perhaps even thousands of years. Unfortunately, Richard had open blisters on his hands and the poison entered his system that way.'

'Poor Margaret.' Shannon shook her head and tears began to flow down her pale cheeks. 'He was a lovely guy you know.' Then the thought sunk in about her own husband and she looked up alarmed. 'So, do you think Jasper was poisoned too?'

'No, no, I'm not thinking that.' Harrison quickly tried to calm her. 'Jasper didn't come into contact with the same objects as his father, so it was impossible for him to have died the same way. I wanted to chat to you about your husband, try to understand what happened to him.'

'They told me it was heart failure. Those things can get passed on in your genes, so I took Zack straight in for tests. He's fine, but they're going to monitor him.'

'That's good news.'

'Yeah,' she said, flatly.

He could see she meant it, but her son would still be without his father, and she was without her husband.

'Tell me about Jasper, what kind of personality was he? Was he confident?'

Shannon looked down and away from her laptop camera for a moment as she fought back more tears.

'He was gentle, like Richard, but I wouldn't say he was

particularly confident. Good at his job, yeah, but he could get stressed quite easily and always took things to heart. He was devastated when Richard died, but after Carole was killed too... He was totally beside himself.'

'Did he believe in the family curse?'

Shannon looked up at Harrison. 'He'd been brought up with the stories. After Carole, he was angry that his dad had caused it all, been so stupid as to reawaken it, he said.' She paused a moment and Harrison let her have time.

'He was right in a way wasn't he? Neither Carole nor Jasper would have been in Yorkshire if it wasn't for Richard digging up those poisonous arrows. Both of them were upset about their father. It *was* a curse Henry Templeton buried, shame he hadn't bloody burned them.' Her flash of anger gave way to more grief.

'I'm sorry,' she'd said, disappearing for a few moments to get some tissues.

'Take your time,' Harrison reassured her.

'You know, he told me that when he was a kid, he used to see a ghost at their house. He was absolutely adamant about it. Believed it was his great grandfather's brother, Edward who haunted the place. He wasn't scared of him, reckoned they used to have conversations, and he said he'd warned him about the curse. So, yeah, he did believe it.'

'Did you speak to him the night he died?'

She nodded and bit her bottom lip.

'Yup. He told me to stay away, keep Zack safe. I was worried about him actually, I should have done something but I didn't know what to do. I couldn't leave Zack and Jasper wouldn't have wanted me to, but I wasn't there to help my husband when he needed me.'

'Why were you worried about him?' Harrison asked gently.

'You know, he was in such a state. He had like a panic attack when he was talking to me, getting breathless. He told me he'd be next. Said the curse might take him too. Kept going on and on about the message that Carole had left on the answerphone.'

'Had he had panic attacks like that before?'

'He said he sometimes got palpitations when he was stressed, but nothing that had made him so breathless. I tried to calm him down, said he was grieving and in shock and asked him to see a doctor and get something to help, valium or something, but he wouldn't listen. We talked for about an hour, I keep trying to persuade him that the curse couldn't be real, that Carole must have been mistaken but I had no answers, no explanations. In the end, he looked so tired I thought he'd sleep. I was going to ring Cee in the morning, she'd come over to be with Margaret, and I hoped she might persuade Jasper to see a doctor. But I was too late. By the morning he was dead.'

'You mustn't think it was your fault,' Harrison told her.

'I don't know what to think anymore,' she'd replied. 'The whole thing is just so unreal. Is Zack in danger?' She looked behind her at the little boy. 'I've moved him into my room, I'm too scared to let him leave my side. We can't live like this. Everywhere I look there's stories about it. It's all over the internet, and those vampires, no one has explained what Carole saw, have they?'

'Not yet, but there will be a logical explanation,' Harrison replied.

'Yeah, I kept trying to persuade Jasper of that, but look what happened to him. If there's a logical explanation, why haven't we heard it? I'm not going to relax until I know our little boy is safe.'

33

Ryan's hunt for the two names that Harrison had given him, wasn't easy. While he knew they existed, could find birth certificates and addresses for them, he couldn't see any evidence of a presence online - at all - which for people of their age was pretty unusual. If it hadn't been for the fact that the reason they had the names in the first place was because Harrison told him they'd come from somebody they were at school with, then he'd have been working along the theory that they might be false identities, or stolen identities.

Once the distraction of Desmond Manning was out of the way, it left him some time to focus on the task. What reason could there be that their names couldn't be found online? Drug dealers was his first guess, but he quickly dismissed that idea because he couldn't find any reason why drug dealers might have links to people dressing up as vampires.

His next thought was people smuggling. The headland could provide an excellent view of incoming boats, and maybe they weren't dressed up as vampires but were somehow in clothing that looked out of place in England and Carole had mistaken it. He'd contemplated the idea, and contacted the National Crime Agency's specialist team. They'd quickly been able to help refute the idea however, when they pointed out Ryan's poor geographical knowledge. Yorkshire wouldn't have been an ideal crossing point for people smugglers as the distance between Europe and the British coast was much greater than in the Channel. That coupled with why they would have all been at the stones and not being driven away quickly from the beach, knocked that idea on the head. He was back to the drawing board.

Then Ryan remembered Harrison's comment that they reminded him of Ryan himself. Geeks the guy in the pub had called them. What online activity could be combined with vampires? He had his eureka moment among the Camarilla as the answer to his quest became so obviously clear, LARPing!

34

Speaking to Shannon Templeton gave Harrison a renewed sense of urgency. He could totally understand why she was being so defensive about their son, and until she got the truth that fear was always going to be there. When he got back to his desk, he found he'd got a missed call from Jack. He called him straight back.

'Just had an update from Gordon, they've charged Manning and he's pleaded guilty. Doesn't want a fuss, apparently. More likely that he doesn't want your mystery man catching wind that he's been arrested. They'll let me know when the sentencing hearing gets scheduled.'

'Thanks Jack,' Harrison said, 'And I'm not sure I properly thanked you for being there yesterday.'

'It's alright mate. I know you'd have done the same for me.' Jack's mind went back to their first case together when Harrison had carried him out of a burning building. He knew he could rely on him. 'Actually, I've got some news,' he added tentatively. 'Marie's pregnant again.'

Harrison heard the hesitation in his friend's voice and

was more than aware of the implications of his good news.

'That's great. She'll be fine this time. They'll monitor her really closely and she won't be able to avoid support. Even if she goes into denial, she's on the system now, and that's if she even gets it again. You said yourself that Daniel's birth had been particularly traumatic for her, the second one is usually easier, she may not have any issues at all.'

'Yeah, you're right. Cheers. I just have to keep on telling myself that. I'm excited about Daniel having a brother or sister, it's what we'd wanted. It's just... well you know.'

'How has Marie taken it?'

'She said she was a little nervous when she first found out, but she's excited. She's positively glowing in fact, looking forward to doing it right, as she puts it, this time round.'

'Well, that's definitely great news Jack, congratulations. Enjoy it.'

'Actually, while you're on the phone, she asked me to ask you something. Well, we wanted to ask actually. Would you and Tanya like to come round for Christmas lunch? Ryan too? I know Tanya has family so she might want to go home, but you're all welcome. We're not going anywhere, we're staying put and it would be good to celebrate with you all. We fancy Christmas at home rather visiting the in laws again. A good traditional lunch with all the trimmings.'

Harrison was lost for words for a few moments. He'd never had a traditional family Christmas lunch before. There'd been versions of it when he'd been with his mother, but she was never a traditionalist. After her death, he'd spent many Christmas days on his own, or sometimes at friends' houses. There'd been a few years where he'd gone round to his old friend, Professor Andrew McKendrick's, but that had always been a group of singletons, mostly grad students. It had been nice, but not like the version he'd occasionally seen in the movies. He was touched.

'Thank you, I'll ask Tanya. I think I'd really like that.'

'Good, I'll ask Ryan then. But Harrison, there's one condition.'

'Oh?'

'Yeah, you have to suspend truth for the day. You're not to start giving us any reality checks as to why we do what we do for our Christmas traditions. For the purposes of Christmas Day you need to just believe in a bit of magic and enjoy it for what it is.'

Harrison heard the smile in Jack's voice.

'I will. I promise,' he replied.

HARRISON'S next appointment was with Lizzie Meyer, Lee Reynold's girlfriend. He didn't know if Lee and Jasper's deaths had any connection, but just knowing that they shared some of the same genetic make-up, raised that possibility.

Lizzie hadn't been working in the hair salon since Lee's death and so Harrison went to meet her at her flat, the one where Lee had frequently stayed over.

Her flat was in a converted house on an estate that was away from the quaint stone buildings of the main road in the village. This was a council built estate with houses that looked like they'd been constructed in the 1970s. They weren't pretty, but they were solid and functional. While it wasn't as plush as Mrs Paulson's bungalow estate, they were clearly well-loved family homes.

Lizzie opened her door to Harrison with pink puffy eyes and the drawn face of the bereaved.

'Sorry about the mess,' she said as she showed him in.

'I've just not had the energy to clean.'

'Please don't worry. I'm really sorry for your loss,' Harrison had said to her, sitting on the sofa she'd shown him to.

Her chin had trembled, and he thought she was about to cry again, but she held it together.

'Do you want a drink?'

'No, I'm fine.'

Lizzie positively crashed onto a chair. It was one she'd clearly spent a great deal of time in because there were tissues, new and used on the little table next to it, and a man's hoody on the arm. Harrison didn't need detective training to realise that was Lee's, and she'd obviously been taking comfort from holding it.

The flat wasn't big, it formed the upper floor of the house and so he guessed it probably only had one bedroom. The room they were in, was a kitchen/diner/lounge. It was decorated simply, and there weren't many ornaments or pictures on the walls, apart from a small montage of photo tiles stuck to the wall. Harrison recognised a younger Lizzie and Lee amid the group shots of friends and family.

'How long were you and Lee together?'

Lizzie took a long, shivery breath before answering.

'We met at school, been together seven years. We were going to get engaged in the new year.'

Harrison felt her loss, a future that had been snatched cruelly from her. Dreams shattered.

'Do you have any idea why? What killed him? No one tells me anything because I'm not his next of kin, just his girlfriend.' She said the last part with some acidic sarcasm in her tone.

'I'm sorry, that must be hard. Are his parents not keeping you informed?'

Lizzie shrugged. 'His mum's alright, but John is too self-obsessed. It's all about him and I'm not family.'

'Well, you know that at present it looks like he suffered heart failure, but we don't have a cause.'

'According to most of the village - it was the bloody Templeton curse.'

'So you knew about Lee's heritage?'

'Yeah, his dad was always on about it. Seemed to think he had some kind of rights as a grandson. Lee couldn't care less, but John wanted to own the Templeton estate and claim his rightful inheritance.' Lizzie's tone was again sarcastic and contemptuous. 'Sorry,' she added. 'I sound really bitter don't I? John can be a prat sometimes. I've heard he's trying to get Lee put in the Templeton tomb. That is just so *not* what he'd have wanted.'

Harrison let her talk.

'His dad is alright, they got on, but he could be quite overbearing at times. Lee would have moved out from home properly if he hadn't kicked up so much fuss. Didn't want his little boy living in an ex council flat. They argued about it and we ended up compromising, but he tried to spend as little time at theirs as possible.'

'Do you know why he chose to go home that night?'

'He was really tired. His dad wanted to talk to him, he'd been ringing him up at work, and so he thought it would be easier just to go home for the night. I was due to go out with my girlfriends anyway and they were coming round here for pre's. I know Lee didn't want to have to answer any questions about the Templetons or listen to anymore gossip about it, so he went home.'

'Did Lee believe in the curse story?'

'Not at first, but yeah, when Carole and Jasper died too, it got to him. Everyone was talking about it. They still are, that's one of the reasons I can't go back to the salon yet. It's all our clients can talk about. Lee started having trouble sleeping, he got really stressed, was pacing up and down the flat worrying about it. Started talking as though he might be next. I even thought he was dying one night, he seemed to pass out, but he said it had just been a fainting fit cos he was so tired.'

'If he was so worried, why didn't he seek medical help? Did you call an ambulance?'

Lizzie looked down at her lap and started tugging at her sleeve.

'You know his dad's a doctor right?'

Harrison nodded.

'Lee loved his rugby. They were due to go up in the league this season. If he'd told his dad what was going on, he'd have banned him from playing, and yeah I know what you're going to say, he's a grown man, he could have ignored his dad, but you don't know John. He'd have put pressure on him and told the club manager. Lee made me promise not to tell anyone, especially his parents.'

Lizzie began to cry again.

'He'd had a few times when he'd got a bit breathless in a match, but he'd covered it up by pretending he had an injury, had pulled something or other. When I asked him about it, he refused to admit it. I thought he was just feeling extra stressed, he was really fit, young. How could he have had a bad heart? I thought that when all the crap about the Templeton curse calmed down, he'd be fine.'

Lizzie broke down completely at that point and Harrison spent half an hour trying to console her. He didn't ask anymore questions. He didn't need to, but he did urgently need to speak to Bob Williams again to ensure that no other families in the village were torn apart by this grief.

35

Harrison rode his bike to Bob's cottage, much to the displeasure of Rebel the cat, who scarpered pretty fast around the back at the sound of the big machine's arrival. Even before Harrison had walked up the front path, Bob had the door open and was waiting for him expectantly.

'I need you to promise me you're not going to talk to any of your colleagues in the press about what we're about to discuss and what I've already told you,' Harrison said to him. 'Not until we've spoken to families. If you do, then not only could you be risking somebody's life, but you'll find yourself in DI Christie's bad books and almost certainly facing a charge.'

'OK, but you've got to offer me something,' Bob countered.

'What? Apart from the knowledge that you could be helping save a life, or lives?' Harrison raised an eyebrow. 'You can get a full interview before anyone else. The double curse of the Templetons would make a good headline.'

'Has a ring to it,' Bob mused, 'you've missed your

vocation Dr Lane. Don't worry I'll keep schtum. Come on in. I'm enjoying the excitement.'

They went through to the kitchen, where Bob had laid out some documents on the kitchen table.

'So, after you phoned, I went through all the Templeton family records, and you were right. There were several early deaths over the years, usually of young men, but not always. Now that wouldn't be something which we'd have particularly thought unusual because of course there were all sorts of things killing people off in the old days, but after what you'd said, I dug out all the death certificates and records of deaths, that I could find. There were several that were registered as being either as a result of a problem with the heart, or they didn't have a clue, the person just dropped dead. The most obvious one of course was poor Edward who I'd told you about before.'

'I thought that might be what you'd find.' Harrison scanned the documents in front of him. 'Can you get me copies of these?'

'Yes sure, and I've got the list of those in the village who are descendants. What would be interesting is to look at their family histories in the last two or three generations and see if they'd had any early deaths, but I haven't had time to do that yet I'm afraid.'

'It's fine, I think what you've given me and what I already know are enough. I'm more concerned now about those who are alive and keeping them that way,' Harrison replied. 'We need to act now.'

36

DI Christie had thankfully just purchased the item at the top of his wife's wish list, when the call came through from Dr Harrison Lane. Within minutes he was on his way back to the station.

When he got there, Harrison had commandeered a white board and was just finishing writing a list of names on it, watched by the rest of his team.

'I'll have to get this agreed from above, so you're going to need to persuade me that this theory of yours is right. I don't get how this could all happen at the same time.'

'OK,' Harrison said and launched straight into it. 'We thought the curse of the Templetons was the poisoned arrowheads, and sure, it was one and certainly the more sensational one; but the real curse of the Templetons is, I believe, a genetic heart condition, some kind of arrhythmia.'

'That's something we'd looked at quite early on.'

'Yes, but we were thrown off the scent of a genetic heart disorder originally because we knew that Richard was definitely OK and yet he'd had a heart attack. Now that we can discount his death because of the poison, we're left with two young men, seemingly healthy, who died of heart failure and share the same genetic heritage. Again, something that we hadn't at first been aware of because Lee wasn't officially a Templeton.'

Adam nodded, concentrating on Harrison's line of thought.

'Bob Williams had told us that Edward Templeton, Henry's brother, died of some kind of heart seizure. Now Edward was already someone who was probably under pressure in society because of his sexuality, so he was already anxious. I suspect that when his adventuring brother returned with tales of cursed temples and his dead travelling companions, it added to Edward's stress - or possibly it was unrelated. But what we do know is that Henry blamed the temple curse for his brother's death and buried the things he'd taken under the blood stone. So that legend was born. The reality is that generations of Templetons had already been impacted by the heart issues. Bob was able to find several other death certificates where it was cited as the reason for early death.'

'But Richard was fine.'

'Yes, because hereditary heart issues are not always passed on, like many genetic diseases, it can be hit and miss as to whether you get it or not. So, we know that Richard didn't inherit it, but it's possible that both Jasper and Lee did. I spoke to Lizzie Meyer earlier, Lee's girlfriend, she told me he'd been having some dizzy spells and feeling breathless. Shannon Templeton described her husband as having what seemed like a panic attack. She said he was breathless and had in the past told her about palpitations when he'd been stressed.'

'OK, so you're saying that it's just a big coincidence that they both died at virtually the same time, and the same time as Richard - even if his death was unconnected?' DI Christie frowned, rubbing his chin with his left hand.

'No. That's the second part of the theory. Have you ever heard of the nocebo effect?'

'Don't you mean placebo?' Sergeant Cutter asked.

'No. I mean nocebo. It's the opposite to placebo. It's where negative expectations result in negative effects.'

DI Christie shrugged and shook his head.

'We have to consider the environment in which both Lee and Jasper were living. Everyone was talking about the Templeton curse, first Richard and then Carole died. Carole's death was particularly bizarre, and the story was in all the media. The whole village has talked of nothing since. Lee's dad was obsessed with the Templetons, and Jasper was devastated by the loss of his father and sister. Both men were aware of, and became afraid of, the Templeton curse. I've had this verified by both Lizzie and Shannon. At some point, they both reached the point where they thought they were going to die next. Now when we're stressed and anxious, our fight and flight response is triggered which releases adrenaline. Adrenaline can cause arrhythmia. When the person feels their heart responding like that it triggers even more adrenaline to be released. So you see a vicious circle is created which puts more and more pressure on the heart. If that heart is already struggling, it's easy to see how it can just fail.'

'So you think that Lee and Jasper literally frightened themselves to death?'

'Yes, somebody said something to me recently which reminded me, there is scientific proof of this nocebo effect. Generally speaking, negative thinking people are likely to die younger than those who think positively. I'd also read a paper on some mass incidences of this which relate to our case. In the 1980s in America, there was a strikingly high number of sudden deaths in young Laotian-Hmong refugees. The phenomena had been reported as far back as the 1950s with Filipino men in Tokyo. What the study found was that these people had a genetic disposition to heart failures, and that they were stressed as they were living in a strange place that didn't support their usual customs and beliefs, with uncertainty about their futures. The stress was elevated by the inability to be able to practise their usual traditional religious ceremonies. In their culture, they had a strong belief in night time attacks by an evil spirit. Without being able to appease the spirits with sacrifices or whatever their belief system required, they thought it would anger them and they would be unprotected. It was a cycle of stress on stress with a faulty heart. Put simply they believed they were at risk and unable to do anything about it and so it happened.'

Harrison watched it all sinking in to the detective's brain and then saw his eyes cross to the whiteboard.

'I got this list from Bob. It's the families that he knows share genetic heritage with the Templetons. We need to contact every family and get them to test for a heart problem and we need to spread the word that this isn't some ancient tribal curse. There could be somebody out there right now who is stressing that they might be next, and if they've got the bad heart gene, then they might be right. What they need is to get medical help, not to appease some evil tribal spirit.'

37

Charlotte had spent most of the day in bed, sleeping fitfully. She thought of nothing else but the curse. What would it look like? Would it seep slowly into her room like some shadowy grim reaper, or charge in on the back of some devilish steed? Would it be some ancient tribal spirit, dancing around her, mocking her before it took her life? Would it be painful? And where would she go? Would she be denied a route to heaven? Would she forever be cursed in some dark fiery hell? When she thought of what was next, that's when her breathing became ragged and she struggled to stay conscious.

When her parents came home from work, her mother was worried about her pallor and weakness, and said she was going to take her to the doctors the next morning. Charlotte wondered if she would survive the night.

She heard the doorbell ring, and a stranger's voice in their hallway, but it wasn't until several pairs of feet came up the stairs and into her room that she really took notice.

A young police woman walked into her room and asked her a couple of questions, but she forgot what she said as soon as the words left her lips. She heard the word ambulance and the fear in her mother's voice. Was she dying now? Was this it?

Charlotte Benson, great granddaughter of Henry Templeton was rushed into intensive care with near heart failure. It would take an operation, and the implanting of a high-tech defibrillator to keep her heart beating as it should, but Charlotte would eventually fully recover and live a long life. She had escaped the Templeton curse.

38

Ryan's message reached Harrison shortly after he'd presented his theory about Jasper and Lee to DI Christie and the team. The incident room had become a hive of activity. Adam had immediately taken their request for extra support to his bosses, and a team of community police officers had been dispatched to speak to families. The press conference scheduled for later that afternoon to announce Richard's cause of death, was now going to be used to ask anyone who thought they might have a genetic link to the Templetons, to seek medical advice.

That left just one death to solve, and it had been the most baffling. Had Carole Templeton really seen vampires, or people dressed as vampires? Or had her mind played tricks on her? Ryan's message came with an address for the lad that Harrison had spoken to in the pub a few nights ago. His visit to David Welsh would finally answer that question.

To say David was nervous, was putting it mildly. He opened the door to the small terraced house, like someone about to face the firing squad. The skinny young man, with jet black hair and tinted glasses looked even paler in the sunlight.

'My mum's out. She doesn't know about any of this,' he said to Harrison. 'Are you going to arrest me?'

'I've come to hear your story, to find out what happened.'

'It wasn't our fault. We weren't doing anything wrong.' He looked as though he might burst into tears at any moment, but stepped back and allowed Harrison into the hallway.

David walked them through into the kitchen, a narrow affair with a small table that was book ended by two chairs. He sat down on one and Harrison pulled up the other.

'You know about LARPing?'

'It's not something I was familiar with,' Harrison replied.

'Live Action Role Playing. It's a mix between gaming, acting, and cosplay. You know where people dress up as characters.'

'Yeah, I'm familiar with that.'

'We play Vampire: The Masquerade, it can be tabletop or you can also do LARP on location. We game online most of the time, but LARPing is more social. It stops our parents moaning that we never go out, and it's a laugh. Usually. That's what we were doing that evening. We didn't know some bloke had just died there. If we had we wouldn't have gone that night. And we didn't see the woman until it was too late.'

'Too late?'

'Yeah, you know she kind of panicked. I guess she must have seen us and yeah we'd look pretty freaky if you didn't know what we were doing. Paul had his full Nosferatu costume on.'

'Did you try to explain to her?'

'Yeah, we tried to shout, go over and tell her, but she just shot off too fast. Then... well, you know.'

'So why didn't you call for help? Why did you leave her to die?'

'We don't take mobile phones. It's one of our rules so that no photos can ever be taken and appear online. Some of us have jobs with the council or law firms so it's purely analog, we just use dice and stuff to play. We tried to help her, but we couldn't reach, she was too far down; so we ran back to the cars to drive and call for help. We'd literally just got back to the car park when we heard the sirens, so we thought that she must have made the call herself and she was going to be OK. So we ran, thinking she'd try to get us arrested for frightening her. It was only later that we heard she hadn't made it.'

'You could still have come forward and explained what happened.'

David looked at Harrison and then away again.

'I know, but we were scared by then, it just blew up so big. We thought we'd be accused of murder or something. Some of us wanted to go to the cops, but others were too worried about people not understanding. Everyone was talking about it. We already get labelled geeks, they might think we were real vampires. We just play games, that's it and we had no idea she was there. We'd never have scared her purposely. I swear.'

HARRISON WAITED until the morning to tell DI Christie about Carole Templeton's unfortunate and tragic end. He wanted the priority to be ensuring that anyone who might have a genetic heart issue was reached by the community police, or the media first. David Welsh's group of LARPers were a bunch of harmless gamers, who happened to be in the wrong place, at the wrong time, and wearing the wrong dress code. It was an accident but one which had yet again been born from her father's unfortunate decision to try to dig up his grandfather's curse.

'I guess I was wrong in one sense,' Harrison told Adam Christie as he prepared to go home the next day. 'I said all the deaths were probably separate, and that we were trying to put them together to form a pattern. In one sense that was true, but in another it wasn't. They *were* all intrinsically interlinked even if they were individual circumstances. Without Richard's first decision and death, the others would almost certainly still be alive. It was a chain of events. Admittedly Lee and Jasper were living on borrowed time, but their heart conditions might have been picked up at some other point.'

DI Christie had struggled to get his head around the concept of LARPing, but he'd agreed with Harrison, that while the group should be warned about not having come forward at the scene of a crime, there would be no charges for them to answer. Carole's death had been a tragic accident born out of the circumstances of the place and time.

'I've just spoken with Ciara O'Donoghue,' Adam said, 'The good news is that Shannon Templeton has agreed to bring her son to see Margaret. He's the only heir now, and just knowing that he's OK and her family's deaths have rational explanations, has given Margaret a reason to carry on. She's due out of hospital today and is eating again. I know she'll never recover from her losses, but at least she can enjoy seeing her grandson grow up.'

'That's good news,' Harrison said.

'I'm just relieved we didn't have a mass murderer on our

hands,' Adam Christie replied, lightening the mood. 'I thought we were in an episode of Midsomer Murders at one point with the number of deaths. I know an accidental death rather than murder, doesn't help the victims' families, it won't bring them back, but at least we can put paid to all the stories of vampires and curses.'

'Not sure that will please Bob and the Reverend.'

'Well, Bob will be fine, he's still got his publishing contract and we've granted an exclusive interview with him this afternoon, as you requested. I believe he's negotiated a nice deal for himself with the Mail reporter. As for the Reverend, the church has served him his notice. It's retirement for his unique brand of fire and brimstone.'

Harrison didn't voice his reaction to that news, but privately he thought that was divine justice.

'I can't thank you enough for helping us sort all this out. If there's anything I can ever do for you, please ask.' DI Christie said to Harrison.

The pair shook hands, and Harrison was just turning to leave when a thought crossed his mind.

'Actually there is something,' Harrison said. 'I could really do with some Christmas gift suggestions for my girlfriend.'

39

Harrison didn't go straight home when he arrived back in London, he headed to the Metropolitan Police headquarters. It was their final day as the Ritualistic Behavioural Crime unit for the Met, and although he and Ryan had already moved most of their stuff out, he wanted to give the place one last look over before they shut the door for the final time. He was surprised to open the door and find the lights still on and Ryan at his desk.

'I knew you'd want to come in one last time.' Ryan smugly smiled.

'I guess it also helps that your phone app can track my every move!' Harrison replied, eyebrows raised.

'It helps,' Ryan smirked as his boss flopped into his office chair with a satisfied sigh.

'Thanks for everything you've done the last few days, I couldn't have done it without you.' Harrison said to him.

Ryan nearly burst with pride and pleasure.

'That's what being a team is all about,' he'd replied. 'Sorry I took so long to come through with the vampires, it was right under my nose. I should have known that gamers never use their real names online, that's why I couldn't find the link initially.'

'You more than came through on everything. Fancy a take out? I'm starving.'

'Do you need to ask?'

The pair of them sat together in their windowless, empty basement office sharing a Chinese takeaway and reminiscing about their first year as the Ritualistic Behavioural Crime unit.

'We've come a long way,' Harrison mused, negotiating a particularly slippery slither of baby corn with his chopsticks. 'Next week is a whole new chapter for us.'

'Yeah, you should see my new computers,' Ryan's eyes widened.

'And you're going to Jack's for Christmas Day?'

Ryan nodded.

'I'll pick you up.'

'What about for you, boss? Personally I mean, do you feel like you can move on?'

Harrison thought for a few moments, shaking his head as Ryan offered him the last sweet and sour chicken ball.

'It's been a roller coaster week of extremes. From finding out my father is the notorious psychopathic killer, Edward Carter, or the Nightingale Killer if you want to use his tabloid name; to discovering my mother was a police informant. Getting Desmond Manning behind bars has definitely ticked some boxes, but I've not caught up with my mother's killer yet and that means my journey isn't over. I'm going to need you to help me track back Carter's movements before he met my mother and while they were together. Maybe there'll be a clue there. I think he had something to do with the mystery man.'

Ryan smiled.

'Knew you'd be asking me that, I've already started.'

'I should have known, cheers Ryan.'

'Actually,' Ryan hesitated, 'there's something I found out which I think you should know,' Ryan stopped eating for a moment and studied his boss's face. 'It will come out at some point, anyway. You've got a half sister and brother.'

'Yeah, but they're from the dark side of my genetics, so I'm not going to be rushing for a nice family reunion with them.' Harrison replied.

'That's true, they're your dad's side, but the bizarre thing is your sister's a forensic psychologist. Works in a prison. Not a doctor or specialist in ritualistic crime like you, but she's a psychologist. Funny that, don't you think?' Ryan added, popping the last sweet n sour ball into his mouth.

Harrison wasn't sure what he felt about that latest piece of family news, but he didn't have long to worry about it. His mobile rang.

'Dr Lane. It's DI Seb Bartholomew at the NCA. Sorry to call you so late and before we've been properly introduced, I know you're not officially joining us until Monday, but we've got a bit of a situation on our hands that requires your unit's specialist talents. Seems we have a pyromaniac serial killer who doesn't take too kindly to Christmas and leaves bizarre clay dolls behind with his victims, like some sick Santa Claus. Don't suppose you could head to Suffolk tomorrow morning could you and check it out?'

BOOK 7: WINTER FIRES

It's Christmas and a time for celebration, but somebody, or something, is delivering murder and mayhem, not goodwill

Churches are being burned down and members of the clergy are being murdered. As Christmas nears, the pace of the killings quicken. Can Dr Harrison Lane, head of the Ritualistic Behavioural Crime unit, find out what is happening and save more than just the festive season?

Follow Dr Harrison Lane and his assistant, Ryan, as they move to the National Crime Agency.

Their first case is to track down a pyromaniac serial killer who hates Christmas and leaves bizarre clay dolls behind with his victims, like a sick Santa Claus.

Winter Fires will also begin Harrison's latest stage of his personal journey, as he tries to find out more about his mother's past and hunt down the mystery man responsible for her murder.

A HARRISON LANE MYSTERY
WINTER FIRES
GWYN GB

THANK YOU FOR BRINGING HARRISON TO LIFE

Thank you so much for choosing to read about Dr Harrison Lane and his Ritualistic Behavioural Crime unit. Six books in and he's only just getting going! Without you, he would still just be a notebook full of ideas and scribbled storylines. Please if you get the opportunity, I would appreciate you leaving a review and welcome any feedback you'd like to share with me on my social pages, or via email.

As with all the Harrison books, I undergo extensive research so that the very clever Dr Lane can solve his crimes in the most realistic way. The poisonous arrowheads were an idea that came to me after watching a documentary about the British Museum and some of their exhibits.

I'd never heard of LARPing before or that there is a hidden group of people who do believe they need to drink human blood! These were revelations I came across while trying to find a reason that Carole Templeton would have seen vampires. With regard to where our stories of vampires come from, the plausible reasons given by Harrison in relation to Simon Mason in the 1700s, are all well documented.

Finally, the nocebo effect is something which I'd read about in terms of how one's attitude to life impacts your health and I was able to link this to proven cases where people who were unfortunate enough to have genetic heart disorders, were literally able to frighten themselves to death.

I'm lucky to be very much a glass half full kind of person and tomorrow is always a new day of fresh opportunity. For me, it will mean a new story to write and I'm working on an exciting new character and series in addition to the next Harrison Lane. Thank you again for reading my stories and I hope tomorrow is a good day for you too.

Gwyn GB

CONNECT WITH GWYN

Visit www.gwyngb.com/harrisonlane if you'd like to join Gwyn's readers' club and receive a FREE novelette telling how Harrison set up the Ritualistic Behavioural Crime unit and his first explosive case.

You will receive news and previews of Gwyn's books as well as competitions and offers. No spam guaranteed and you can unsubscribe any time.

You can connect with Gwyn online. She'd love to hear from you:

Gwyngb.com
Email: gwyn@gwyngb.com

Or join in the conversation on my social channels and follow me on Amazon for book release updates:

facebook.com/GwynGBwriter
twitter.com/GwynGB
instagram.com/gwyngb
bookbub.com/authors/gwyn-gb
tiktok.com/@gwyngbauthor
amazon.com/author/gwyngb

Printed in Great Britain
by Amazon

86898013R00140